BOOK 4

VOW

BY J.D. CRIST

Dedication

I am still in awe of those who have inspired me to keep telling Emily's story. It has continued to grow in ways that surprise even me as I watch the words appear. To every one of you, I am truly blessed to have you in my life.

Trigger Warnings

This book explores several themes and topics that may be uncomfortable for some readers. These include:

Death

Zombies

Killing

Blood

Strong Language

Miscarriage

Child Abuse

If you are unable to continue, I understand. But if you are, welcome back to the world of The Dead Flash.

.

Chapter 1

Emily walked down the main street without realizing she was rubbing her stomach. She and Shawn hadn't told anyone about the pregnancy yet. They had talked about it and decided to keep it between them until after the wedding. That would put them over the three month mark and let them enjoy their secret a little longer. She was used to not talking about her pregnancy with anyone but Marley. So, this was not out of the norm for her. However, she was not used to hiding the small movements that would give her away.

"You feeling alright?" Christine asked as she walked up beside her.

"Yeah," Emily smiled back at her. "Just a little tired."

"Is your stomach upset?" Christine asked with concern.

"A little," Emily quickly replied as she realized what she was doing. "I'll be fine, though."

"If you're not feeling well, you should get some rest," Christine said in her comforting mom's voice.

"I'm just doing a quick check-in and then working in my office," Emily smiled at her. "Nothing too bad today."

"Alright," Christine nodded with a look of concern. "If you need anything, just let me know."

"I will, Mom," Emily assured her. "If you want to stop by later, I'm trying to finish some wedding stuff."

"I finish work at three," Christine said, looking excited.

"Your sister and I can come by once we are done."

"You know where to find me," Emily grinned.

Christine turned and quickly took off towards the school. Emily hoped that she had not given away the pregnancy secret. She was pulled out of her thoughts by Marley licking at her fingers. She reached down and rubbed his head. At least she didn't have to hide the secret from him.

She turned and continued her walk up the main street with Marley. She made her regular check-ins with each department head, and everything seemed to be running smoothly. She invited Jessica, Julia, and Sarah to the wedding meeting. Each of them seemed just as excited as her mom. She made her way to the town hall and settled behind her desk while Marley took his place on the floor for his morning nap.

She worked her way through the reports as the hours quickly passed. She did not realize how much time had gone by until she heard familiar footsteps approaching her office door.

She promptly closed up the reports and cleared the center of the desk.

"How are you feeling today?" Shawn smiled as he walked through the door carrying their lunch.

"Happy," Emily smiled back at him.

"And the baby?" Shawn asked as he set down the food and took a seat.

"Fine," Emily assured him. "I almost gave away that we were pregnant earlier."

"Who'd you almost tell?" Shawn laughed as he took a bite of his sandwich.

"I was rubbing my stomach without realizing it, and my mom saw," Emily admitted as she began to eat. "I told her."

I was tired and had an upset stomach."

"That explains why she told me to make sure you rest," Shawn smiled.

"She and Rachael are going to stop by later and help me finish some of the wedding details," Emily continued.

"Are we still planning on August twenty-eighth?" Shawn asked.

"If it's okay with you," Emily nodded.

"You could tell me it's in an hour, and I'll be fine with it," Shawn grinned at her. "I'm ready to get married to you now."

"I know," Emily said softly. "And I was ready to marry you yesterday. I just want to make sure we do it right."

"You make whatever plans you need to,"
Shawn said, taking her hand. "You just tell me
what to do and when to be there."

"Deal," Emily said, squeezing his hand
back.

She and Shawn continued their small talk
while they finished their lunch.

"I'd better get back to work," Shawn said
as he stood up. "I'll pick up Hope and take care
of dinner tonight. You just get done with what
you need to make the wedding happen."

"If I'm not home in time, you guys go
ahead and eat without me," Emily smiled back.
"You know how women can be when talking
about wedding stuff."

"I've never witnessed it myself," Shawn
admitted. "But I can imagine."

Shawn kissed her head and smiled at her
as he walked out of the office. She continued
her work for a few more hours and then did her
final check-ins with everyone. She then made
her way back to the office just before three. This
time, she decided to sit on the couch to meet
with everyone. Sure enough, everyone came in
just after three. Each of them talked excitedly as
they sat down.

"I have so many ideas, but I'm not sure
what we can and can not do," Christine said,
settling everyone into the task.

"I spoke with Margaret," Jessica spoke
next. "There was an old wedding dress in one of

the houses. She is fixing it up and will adjust it to fit Emily."

"Father Nathan says he's ready to do the service," Emily said after making a mental note to have Margaret fit her dress as close to the date as possible. "I thought we would have the reception on the main street like other gatherings."

"I'll take care of the cake, and everyone will be willing to contribute to the reception's food, " Julia said.

"What about bridesmaids and groomsmen?" Rachael asked.

"I was hoping all of you would be willing," Emily smiled. "It's a lot to ask because you would have to make your dress."

"Yes!" Rachael, Jessica, Julia, and Sarah all said at once.

"I'll have to talk to Shawn about picking four groomsmen," Emily continued.

"What about a honeymoon?" Christine asked.

The room fell silent as the idea of a honeymoon was something none had considered. It seemed impossible to do inside Sanctuary. It wasn't like they could take a vacation outside the wall.

"I don't think a honeymoon is in the cards for us," Emily admitted. "It's no big deal, though. We can just stay home and take a few days off work."

"I wish we could figure something else out for you guys," Christine said with sorrow.

"I agree," Julia spoke up. "You guys deserve a little getaway."

"We don't care about stuff like that," Emily assured them. "We will be hungry, though."

"I'll do a sign-up sheet this week and ensure we have everything covered," Rachael assured her. "If you girls want to come by the shop, I saw a few dresses I think we can fix up nice."

"Sounds good," Sarah smiled.

"You can also have Shawn send the guys by, and we will get them fixed up."

"Any credits can be charged to me for this stuff," Emily said without thinking.

"I think the basics need to be credit-free," Jessica said slowly.

"And any upgrades, personalization, and stuff we can pay for," Rachael said.

"I don't want anyone to have to pay for this stuff," Emily said, a little startled.

"Your dad will insist on paying for anything needed on the dress," Christine said.

"No use in fighting it," Sarah laughed. "We are not letting you pay for it."

"Well, I tried," Emily smiled, admitting defeat. "But if it becomes too much...."

"We won't let you know," Christine smiled. "We got this."

Everyone laughed, and they continued to work through the rest of the small details. The sun was already setting by the time they were finished. She walked out with Marley and made her way home. She opened the door and waited as Marley followed her inside.

"Honey!" Emily called out. "I'm home."

"In the kitchen, dear," Shawn hollered back.

She laughed as she walked to the kitchen and found Shawn setting a plate on the table.

"Dinners ready," Shawn said as he pulled out her chair.

"Thank you," Emily smiled as she sat down. "I'm starving."

"Did you get everything done?" Shawn asked as he sat down beside her.

"I think we have it all planned," Emily smiled at him. "We need you to pick four groomsmen and send them to Rachael to get their outfits."

"I will get that done tomorrow," Shawn said.

"Margaret is making my dress, and everyone insists on helping with food and decorations."

"Sounds like you got it all under control," Shawn nodded.

"Mom was upset that we couldn't go on a honeymoon," Emily continued. "I told her we didn't care about stuff like that."

"I'll take care of it," Shawn said without hesitation.

"What do you mean?" Emily asked, confused.

"I'll take care of our honeymoon," Shawn repeated. "I have an idea of a place that you and I can go for a week that's safe and secluded."

"Where?" Emily asked, putting down her fork on her empty plate.

"I'll take care of it," Shawn smiled as he grabbed her plate and walked to the sink.

"Mommy!" Hope yelled as she ran into the kitchen and hugged her.

"Hey, honey," Emily replied as she pulled Hope into her lap.

"What are you guys talking about?" Hope asked, smiling.

"Daddy is keeping secrets," Emily said, glaring at Shawn.

"It's a wedding present for Mommy," Shawn replied, not even turning around.

"Presents must be kept secret until it's time to open them," Hope scolded her. "You know that."

"But I want to know now," Emily playfully whined.

"If you whine," Hope said in her most grown-up voice, "then you won't get a present at all."

She tried her best to pout while Shawn laughed loudly.

"Yes, ma'am," Emily said, trying not to smile.

"Good mommy," Hope laughed as she patted her on top of her head.

"That's it," Emily said as she quickly began tickling Hope.

"I'm sorry," Hope squealed as she tried to get away from Emily.

"Pat me on the head like you do, Marley," Emily laughed as she continued to tickle Hope.

"Alright, you two," Shawn laughed. "It's time for Hope to get ready for bed."

She stopped tickling Hope and pulled her into a hug.

"You go get ready, and I'll be up to tuck you in," Emily said to Hope.

"Yes, mommy," Hope smiled as she jumped down and made her way out of the room with Marley behind her.

"So," Emily began, "About this honeymoon plan."

"Still a secret present," Shawn smiled as he began to walk out of the kitchen. "Ask again, and I'll tell Hope on you."

"You wouldn't," Emily said, shocked.

"Try me," Shawn replied as he walked out of the room.

"Please don't tell," Emily said as she stood up and ran after Shawn. "I promise I'll be good."

"Don't make a promise you can't keep," Shawn grinned.

"We both know you're still trying to figure it out."

"I promise I'll be good tonight," Emily replied.

"That sounds about right," Shawn laughed.

"I'm ready!" Hope's voice rang out upstairs.

"You get her tucked in, and I'll be back in a bit," Shawn said as he pulled her in a hug. "Veronica is on night shift tonight, and I want to ensure she shows up."

"You need me to come?" Emily asked as she hugged Shawn back.

"I think I can handle it," Shawn said as he let go of her. "I shouldn't be long."

"Alright," Emily said as she leaned up to kiss Shawn. "I'll see you later."

"I love you," Shawn said after kissing her and walking towards the door.

"I love you too," Emily replied.

"Love you, Daddy!" Hope yelled down.

"Love you, Hope!" Shawn hollered back as he walked out the door.

She made her way upstairs and found Hope and Marley were already in bed.

"Do you want to read a story tonight?" Emily asked as she walked in and sat beside them.

"Could we just talk?" Hope asked sheepishly.

"Sure," Emily nodded. "What's on your mind?"

"My father," Hope said, looking down at her hands.

"What about him?" Emily asked.

While she wasn't thrilled to be talking about Chad, she had sworn not to let her feelings dictate what kind of relationship Hope would have with him. She wanted to let Hope make that decision for herself.

"I know he was a bad husband, but maybe he can be a good father," Hope said, twisting the blanket in her hands.

"Hope," Emily said, grabbing her little hands. "If you want to spend time with your father, Daddy and I are perfectly okay with that."

"I don't want Daddy to think I don't love him anymore," Hope admitted. "Or to hurt you by talking to him."

"We love you and want you to do what makes you happy," Emily assured her. "Remember, all we ask is that you don't go alone for the first few visits."

"Just to make sure I'm safe, right?" Hope asked.

"That and to keep me from going crazy," Emily smiled.

"Can you ask him if he wants to have lunch at Julia's tomorrow?" Hope asked.

"I will ask him first thing in the morning," Emily assured her.

"What should I call him?" Hope asked. "Dad doesn't seem right because I don't know him."

"You can call him Dad or Chad," Emily suggested. "Whatever makes you comfortable." "I think I'll call him Chad right now," Hope said after a moment. "You don't think he'll be mad, do you?"

"Of course not," Emily assured her. "I'll explain it to him when I invite him to lunch tomorrow."

"And since Julia would be there, do you and Daddy still need to come?" Hope asked.

She suddenly realized that Hope had chosen her location wisely. It was somewhere where she could still have a trusted adult without her or Shawn being there.

"I'll ask Julia, and if she's okay with it, so am I," Emily nodded. "I would still want you to take Marley."

"Yes, ma'am," Hope nodded.

"Alright," Emily replied. "I think it's time for you to get some sleep.

"Good night, mommy," Hope said as she snuggled under the blanket.

"Good night," Emily said as she kissed Hope's forehead.

"I love you."

"I love you too," Hope replied softly.

She made her way across the room, shut off the light, and closed the door. That was not the conversation that she expected to have that night. She knew that it would happen, but still wasn't ready. She made her way to her room and decided to take a shower while she waited for Shawn to get home. She tried to relax and not dwell too much on Hope wanting to have lunch with Chad. Either possible outcome of the invite worried her. Either Chad would reject Hope, or he would say yes.

"Emily," Shawn's voice rang out over the radio just as she stepped out of the shower.

"Go ahead," Emily replied as she wrapped a towel around herself.

"I may have been wrong," Shawn's voice came back. "Are you able to come to the wall?"

"Yeah," Emily said, frustrated. "I'll be there in a few.

She quickly dried off, threw on some clothes, and ran a brush through her hair. She headed out the door after ensuring the baby monitor was set up. She cursed as she walked to the wall and up the stairs.

"I'm not trying to cause trouble," Chad's voice rang out. "I knew the shift had to be covered, and that's why I'm here."

"But she is required to take a shift," Shawn said calmly, but she knew he wanted to yell.

"What's going on?" Emily asked as she reached the top of the stairs.

"Veronica said she was too tired from work and told Chad to cover her shift," Shawn explained. "I told her earlier that it was unacceptable and she was required to be here."

"Chad, you look exhausted," Emily said, looking at him.

"Exactly," Shawn replied. "And he has his shift in the morning. If he doesn't stop covering for her, he will get so tired he might just fall off this wall!"

"Since when do you care?" Chad spat at Shawn.

"I don't," Shawn admitted. "But it's my job to ensure everyone here is safe. And Hope will be devastated."

Chad looked down at the ground. She could tell that Shawn bringing up Hope had hurt him.

"Go home and tell Veronica you're not taking her shift," Emily said to Chad. "You have your shift in the morning and a lunch date with Hope."

Both Shawn and Chad looked at her with surprise.

"She would like you to meet her at Julia's bakery for lunch," Emily continued. "You must understand she will have Marley with her and, for now at least, she wants to call you Chad."

"She said all of this?" Chad finally spoke.

"Yes," Emily nodded. "She asked me when I tucked her into bed. She was worried you would be upset that she wasn't ready to call you dad. You were a terrible husband, and I'm praying you can be a better father."

"He better be," Shawn snarled at Chad. "If she gets hurt…."

"I know," Chad said after swallowing hard. "I'll be there."

"Just you," Emily emphasized.

"Just me," Chad assured her as he turned to head down the stairs.

Shawn wrapped his arms around Emily as Chad left.

"I'm proud of you," Shawn said once Chad was gone. "I know it's not easy for you to let her spend time with him."

"It's not," Emily agreed. "But I have to let her decide for herself."

"And you know that an army has her back if he steps one toe out of line," Shawn added.

"That helps," Emily smiled.

After several minutes, Veronica came stomping up the stairs. Shawn told her she would just be watching monitors for the night and then turned to leave with Emily.

"I can't believe you dangled that little girl in front of him just to force me to come up here," Veronica snarled at Emily.

"I just delivered the message," Emily replied as she left with Shawn.

Chapter 2

Hope woke early the following day, even for her. She was used to not sleeping in on Saturdays, but getting up even earlier than she did during the week was too much. She felt like she was moving in slow motion as Hope ran through the house, getting ready and doing her chores. It seemed almost like she was afraid she wouldn't be prepared in time for her lunch date.

"Anything else, mommy?" Hope asked as she ran back into the kitchen while Emily sipped her coffee.

"Not that I can think of," Emily admitted. "I think you even did my chores."

"How much longer until lunch?" Hope asked with excitement.

"About six hours," Emily smiled back at her.

"She's got time to re-shingle the roof and clean the gutters at the speed she's working today," Shawn said as he walked into the kitchen, yawning.

"I'm just excited," Hope smiled. "Maybe it will be different talking to him without her around."

"I have to admit," Shawn said as he

poured himself a cup of coffee, "It's been a few weeks since I've wanted to punch him in the face."

"See," Hope said, clapping her hands and jumping up and down. "Even daddy likes him."

"Let's not get carried away there, kiddo," Shawn corrected her. "I'm not awake enough for that."

"Yes, daddy," Hope smiled.

"Why don't you go read for a while?" Emily suggested.

"Great idea," Hope smiled as she ran out of the kitchen.

"I swear if he hurts her…." Shawn began.

"I get the first shot and you second," Emily interrupted.

"Deal," Shawn nodded.

"If you got things here, Julia is probably in the bakery by now," Emily said, setting her coffee cup in the sink. "I need to go talk to her about the lunch date."

"What do I have her do when she's done reading all the books in the house in ten minutes?" Shawn asked as she walked out of the room.

"Shingles or gutters," Emily laughed. "Your choice."

She made her way to the front door with Marley right behind her. It didn't take them long to reach the bakery, where Julia was already working hard.

"It smells amazing here," Emily smiled as she walked in.

"What are you doing up this early?" Julia asked as she turned around and smiled at Emily.

"Hope is excited and got us up," Emily laughed.

"What's got her so excited?" Julia asked as she pulled loaves of bread out of the oven.

"She invited Chad on a lunch date, and he agreed," Emily explained.

"You okay with that?" Julia asked, looking at Emily knowingly.

"Not at all," Emily admitted. "But I have to let her get to know him for herself. There is a small chance that he will be a good dad."

"Very small," Julia added. "I'm surprised Shawn is okay with him coming to your house." "Well, that's why I'm here," Emily began. "We told Hope she couldn't meet him alone, and she asked if they could have lunch here."

"So, she wants him oven-roasted if he gets out of line?" Julia asked.

"Fine with me," Emily laughed. "I just wanted to make sure you would be okay with it. She doesn't want Shawn or me there, but she will have Marley."

"I'll make sure she's good and that she waits for one of you to pick her up after," Julia smiled.

"Thank you," Emily sighed in relief. "I'm probably going to be across the street watching the whole time, but knowing you are watching makes me feel so much better."

"Of course," Julia smiled. "I'll hold him down so you can run over, kick him several times, and then we'll throw him in the oven."

Julia and both laughed. She felt a little bit of her anxiety melt away about the lunch date, but not much. She said goodbye to Julia and headed back home. She realized that she had been in the bakery longer than she thought. Everyone in town started to wake up, and other people were in the street.

"Emily!" Chad called as he ran towards her. "I'm on my way to the wall, but I get off at twelve. What time does Hope want to meet?" "She will be at the bakery at twelve," Emily replied as pleasantly as she could.

"Are you or Shawn going to be with her?" Chad asked, looking around for Shawn.

"Not inside," Emily replied. "Julia will be there along with Marley to watch over things. She will watch Hope until one of us comes to pick her up."

"I wanted to get her a present," Chad smiled. "But then I realized I didn't know what she likes. Any suggestions?"

"I'd skip the present today," Emily forced herself to smile back. "Get to know her now, and then you will be able to give her things that truly mean something."

"That's great advice," Chad nodded. "You're really good at this mom thing."

"It's easy with a kid like her," Emily smiled. "You'd better get going. You don't want to be late."

"Right," Chad said as he began to walk towards the wall.

She couldn't help but feel relieved that the conversation was over as she began to walk home.

"Hey, Emily!" Chad called after her.

She turned back to look at him.

"Thanks for this," Chad said as he waved and began walking again.

She forced herself to wave back with a smile before beginning to walk home again. For some reason, seeing him happy and thanking her made her angry. He had been a horrible person before the flash. He had used and mentally abused her for almost their entire marriage. He mocked her for her miscarriage and now was thanking her. He would never get close to Hope if she forbade it like she wanted to.

"But it's not up to me," Emily said to herself as she walked up the porch stairs. "You'll make sure she's safe, right?" She asked, looking down at Marley.

The look in his dark brown eyes told her that he understood. She patted him on the head and opened the front door. Inside, Shawn sat on the couch and pulled her down next to him.

"Everything all set?" he asked.

"Yeah," Emily replied. "Maybe we should tell her he ran away?"

"She'll be fine," Shawn insisted. "If anything starts, Julia will shut it down fast, and it will only take about ten seconds to get inside.

"What about you?" Emily asked, looking at him.

"I'm giving you a thirty-second head start, then I'm coming in," Shawn laughed. "But I think we both know that today will be fine. He won't try anything on the first visit."

"I hope not," Emily replied.

She sat with Shawn until he headed out to check on the wall and probably give Chad another reminder to behave. She spent a few hours with Hope as she changed her outfit several times to find the perfect one. Before long, it was time for them to head to the bakery.

"You just go inside and sit where Julia tells you," Emily told Hope as they walked.

"You're really not coming in?" Hope asked, looking up at her.

"Not unless you have changed your mind and want me to," Emily smiled back.

"I'll be okay, mommy," Hope insisted.

"You keep Marley with you no matter what," Emily reminded her. "You don't send him away, and you don't leave the bakery for any reason."

"What if there's a fire?" Hope smiled up at her.

"You stand there and try to save that table," Emily teased.

"Yeah, right!" Hope laughed.

She and Hope stopped with Marley just outside the bakery.

"He finishes his wall shift in a few minutes and will come straight here," Emily assured her. "You ready?"

"Ready," Hope nodded.

"Alright," Emily smiled, trying to hold back tears. "You get on inside, and I'll be back in about an hour to pick you up."

"Yes, ma'am," Hope smiled as she turned to walk in.

"Come on, Marley."

Marley didn't hesitate as he followed Hope inside. She watched from the door as Julia led Hope to a table and waved at her. She waved back and slowly made her way across the street. She stood motionless and watched as Chad walked into the bakery a few minutes later. She had a clear view of them from where she stood. Julia had to have done that on purpose. She watched as Chad sat down and could see how happy Hope was.

She turned and began to slowly walk down the street. She knew Hope would see her if she stood there too long. She planned to walk by every five to ten minutes just to check on Hope.

"You really went through with it," Veronica said, stepping in front of her. "He has a

wife and a son at home, but instead, he is having lunch he can't afford with your daughter." "I'm paying for the lunch," Emily smiled.
"She is his daughter, too."

"I see no proof of that," Veronica spat back. "You probably got knocked up after the flash and decided it was less shameful to say it belonged to your husband. Your husband, whom you were separated from after the flash."

"Yes, you caught me," Emily said in disbelief. "And just to keep the sympathy going, I told them how he cheated on me and decided to go be with the woman he knocked up." "I gave him something you couldn't!" Veronica yelled. "You couldn't have children!
Now you are trying to steal him back!"

"I don't want him!" Emily yelled. "I'm getting married, or is that another part of my plan?!"

She looked around and could feel her face was hot with anger. Everyone on the street had stopped and was staring at them. She couldn't help but feel embarrassed.

"Whatever crazy scenarios you've worked out in your head for this drama," Emily said in a normal tone, "You can leave me out of it."

With that, she turned and stormed away from Veronica. She glanced into the bakery as she stormed past and saw Hope laughing. She felt her anger drift away slightly at the sight. If Veronica wanted to be mad, there was nothing she could do about it. She didn't have to let

Veronica control her mood, though. If Veronica wanted to live out this drama, she would have to do it alone. She had too many good things in her life to let Veronica try to spoil them. She set herself to picking up things they needed at home and other busy work. She only passed by the bakery a few times, and each time Hope seemed happy. She waited until nearly two before she entered to pick up Hope.

"I'm sorry," Hope was saying to Chad. "I'm just not ready for that."

"No pressure," Chad replied. "I just know she would like a chance to get to know you."

She instantly knew that Chad was asking Hope to spend time with Veronica. She was already having a hard time letting go enough to let Hope get to know Chad. Veronica was another story. But since Hope was saying no, this was not something she had to worry about.

"You ready?" Emily asked as she walked towards the table.

"Has it been an hour already?" Hope asked, looking around.

"Almost two," Emily smiled back. "I'm sure Chad would be willing to meet you another day so you guys can keep talking."

"Of course," Chad smiled. "Actually, Em, could I talk to you for a second?"

"Sure," Emily forced herself to reply with a smile. "Hope, why don't you take Marley outside? I'm sure he needs to stretch his legs."

"Yes, ma'am," Hope smiled as she stood up. "Bye, Chad."

"Bye, sweetie," Chad yelled back.

She and Chad both watched as Hope left before turning towards each other.

"So," Emily said awkwardly.

"I want to start by thanking you again for today. I realize that how I behaved when we first got here took away my right to ask for things like this," Chad said, looking more at the floor than at her.

"It's no secret that I don't like you," Emily replied. "And Veronica…well, I like you more than her. But this is Hope's choice, and I will support whatever she chooses."

"I wanted to see if I could push my luck and maybe ask for a little bit more," Chad said, looking at her.

"Things are not working out with Veronica," Chad began. "I thought I could come and stay with you for a while. Give me a chance to get to know Hope better and a break from Veronica to figure things out."

She stood in shock for a moment, unable to speak. While she had a spare room, there was no way she would allow her abusive, cheating ex-husband to move in. And wasn't he just asking Hope to spend time with Veronica? She couldn't understand what was happening.

"I don't think that's a good idea," she finally said. "Shawn and I are busy getting ready for the wedding, and I just don't think the

tension in the house would be good for anyone."
"You mean between Shawn and me?" Chad
asked.

"Yeah," Emily replied. "And between you
and me."

"Maybe Shawn could move out for a
while," Chad replied. "Let you, me, and Hope
live together for a while to see if we can make it
work as a family before you get married."
"What?!" Emily asked, shocked.

"We deserve that chance, Em," Chad said,
taking a step closer. "At least give it a chance
before you run off and marry some other guy,
for Hope's sake."

"I will never be with you again!" Emily
heard herself reply forcefully while taking a
step back. "Hope wants to get to know you and
let you be part of her life, fine. But what I do
and who I'm with are none of your business."

She suddenly remembered her fight with
Veronica earlier.

"Your current wife already knows your
plan," Emily blurted out. "And for some reason,
she thinks it's all my idea!"

"She's just upset because she knows it's
not working out between her and me," Chad
replied. "Things are not easy with her, Em, not
like it was with you."

"Not like it was when you used me as
your personal slave?!" Emily replied. "Because
the second I stood up to you stepped out. You'd

better stop this, Chad, before you end up completely alone for the rest of your life."

"I wasn't trying to upset you," Chad said with a look of shame.

She knew he looked genuinely remorseful to everyone else, but she knew that look. It was the same one he used to get her back to being compliant when they were married.

"I'll let you know when Hope would like to meet again," She said, rolling her eyes in frustration. "Until then, you stay away from us."

With that, she turned and walked out of the bakery. Hope was standing with her back towards the bakery, talking to Shawn. Shawn nodded and smiled, but she could tell he had just watched what happened.

"Why don't you run on home, and we'll be right behind you?" Shawn said to Hope.

"Come on, Marley!" Hope squealed as she took off running with Marley right behind her.

"What was that about?" Shawn asked, eyeing Chad as he left the bakery.

"Same Chad, different world," Emily replied, glaring at Chad.

"Are you okay?" Shawn asked, looking at Emily.

"I'm fine," Emily sighed. "He's crazy, but I'm fine."

"Maybe this lunch date wasn't such a good idea," Shawn said, pulling her close.

"It is for Hope," Emily sighed. "But if he doesn't back off me...."

"If he doesn't back off, he's going to have a whole new problem on his hands," Shawn finished for her.

"I just want to go home, lock the door, and relax," Emily sighed.

"I can handle that," Shawn laughed as he scooped her up and ran towards the house.

"What are you doing?!" Emily laughed as she clung to his neck.

"Open the door!" Shawn yelled to Hope as he neared the house.

Hope turned back to see Shawn running while carrying Emily. Hope quickly opened the door and stepped inside. Emily was still laughing as Shawn ran inside.

"Quick, close it!" Shawn called back to her.

"What's going on?" Hope laughed as she quickly ran in and closed the door.

"Lock it quick before she changes her mind," Shawn smiled back, still holding Emily. "Mommy said she wanted to come home, lock the door, and spend the rest of the day with just us."

"No work!" Hope said with excitement while locking the door.

"No work," Shawn grinned as he set Emily down.

"Unless they call me on the walkie." Emily interrupted their celebration.

"What walkie?" Shawn asked with a big grin.

She reached down to her waist and didn't feel the walkie where it should have been.

"Give it back," Emily said, holding her hand to Shawn.

"This is Emily," Shawn said into the walkie in a high-pitched, squeaky voice.

"Give it back," Emily laughed, trying to jump up and take the walkie back from him.

"I'm taking the rest of the day off to spend with my super cute daughter and a hunk of a man," Shawn continued.

"Shawn!" Emily laughed, still trying to get the walkie.

"Got it, Shawn," Sarah replied. "Emily is officially off duty."

"Thank you," Shawn replied in his highpitched voice.

"You know I'm going to tell her you weren't serious," Emily said, putting her hands on her hips.

"How do you plan to do that?" Shawn grinned at her and then looked at Hope. "Run!" Shawn called to Hope as he tossed her the walkie.

Hope caught the walkie and took off as fast as she could. Emily turned to catch her but found her path blocked by Shawn.

"Hide it somewhere she'll never look!" Shawn yelled to Hope as she ran upstairs.

"I know the perfect spot!" Hope yelled back.

Emily wrestled with Shawn for a few minutes before Hope returned.

"It's done!" Hope announced with pride.

"You little traitor," Emily smiled as she lunged at Hope.

"Daddy, help!" Hope yelled as she began to flee.

The house was filled with laughter and playing for the rest of the afternoon. She forgot about the drama outside her door and the nightmare outside the wall.

Chapter 3

Emily kept her distance from Chad and Veronica over the next few weeks. Hope visited with Chad a few more times, but she arranged for Shawn to be the one to pick her up. Shawn hadn't questioned it when she asked, and she couldn't help but feel that he knew the reason why. Hope's visits seemed to be going better and better. She had even begun talking about being ready to speak to Veronica. She had pushed this off and told her just to focus on Chad right now.

The wedding plans had begun to take shape all around town. Shawn kept his secret about the honeymoon destination, but that didn't mean Emily had given up trying to find out. Something she was still trying to do this morning.

"Is it somewhere close?" Emily asked as she followed Shawn up the wall. "We could just make one of the empty homes into a resort."

"You never give up," Shawn laughed.

"Nope," Emily smiled. "And it's one of the things you love about me."

"That it is," Shawn said, shaking his head. "But I need to get to work."

"I'll go with you," Emily smiled.

"Looks like it might rain," Shawn said, looking up at the sky. "The last thing we need is for you to slip up here."

She knew he was worried not only about her but the baby. He would have wrapped her in bubble wrap by now if he could.

"I'll go back down if you give me a hint," Emily teased.

"Two hours," Shawn replied as he turned to walk away.

"Two hours?!" Emily yelled back. "What's that supposed to mean?"

"That's your only hint," Shawn smiled back at her.

"Two hours," Emily repeated to Marley as they headed back down the stairs. "Any ideas?"

Marley looked back up at her with a blank expression on his face.

"It's okay," Emily assured him as she patted him on the head. "I'll figure it out."

She and Marley were still near the top of the stairs when a gust of wind ripped over the wall. She paused and found it difficult to steady herself. After a few moments, the wind died down, and she looked up at the sky. Shawn was right, a storm was coming, and it looked to be a bad one. She quickly descended the stairs, feeling safer with her feet on the ground.

She made her way through Sanctuary, ensuring everyone was ready for the coming storm. She had no way of knowing how bad it would be if it would be bad, but she decided it was best to prepare for the worst. She spent much of the afternoon at the farm, helping Jacob ensure the animals were inside and cared for.

It was nearing dinner time before she headed home. The sky was already dark, and flashes of lightning could be seen. The streets were already empty, and it was just her and Marley. She had not seen Sanctuary look this empty since it had just been her and Marley. She began to walk as fast as possible, her muscles sore from a day of farm work.

They were nearly home when the sky let loose. The rain began to fall in large drops around her, instantly soaking the ground. She felt the cold rainwater on her clothes as they began to stick to her skin. Marley moved quickly to keep up with her as she ran towards the house. She felt herself suddenly stop just in front of the walk. Marley looked up, confused, but remained next to her. She looked at the sky and allowed the cold rain to fall freely on her face.

"Emily!" Shawn called to her from the door. "What are you doing?!"

She looked at him as a smile spread across her face. She had been growing as a person since the flash, but she felt free for the first time since she was a child. She could see the confusion on Shawn's face as he walked toward her. Emily looked down at Marley, still smiling.

"Let's play," Emily said to him as the thunder boomed overhead.

Marley's tail began to wag as she spoke. She looked back at Shawn, who was only a few steps away. Hope now stood in the door, seeming just as confused as he was.

"Catch me if you can," Emily smiled at Shawn.

Shawn paused, more confused than before. She didn't hesitate as she turned and began to run up the main street. The rain was falling hard and had already started to puddle. She made no effort to miss the puddles and instead ran straight through them. The cold water splashed up onto her legs and soaked into her shoes. Marley ran right beside her, helping to splash the water up even more.

She looked over her shoulder to see that Shawn had accepted the challenge and was chasing after her. She ran as fast as she could, but Shawn quickly caught her.

"What are you doing?" Shawn laughed as he wrapped her in his arms.

"You never played in the rain?" Emily laughed back at him.

"Not in a thunderstorm," Shawn replied, water pouring down his face. "Everyone's going to think you've finally cracked."

"Then maybe they should come out and join me," Emily smiled, pulling away from Shawn.

She held her arms out to the side and spun around in the rain, feeling like a child again. When she stopped, she saw Hope had joined them and was turning just like she was.

"You're it," Emily laughed as she tagged Shawn on his chest.

Hope knew this game and instantly took off running. Emily and Marley followed right behind her. She looked over her shoulder and saw that Shawn had decided to play. They ran for several minutes, tagging each other and even Marley a few times.

"Don't you have the sense to come in out of the rain?" Joe's voice rang out as he ran towards them.

"The sense but not the desire," Emily laughed back.

"You know you're going to catch a cold," Rachael added as she joined them.

"Probably," Emily nodded. "But it's worth it."

She looked over at Hope and winked. Hope understood what she was trying to tell her. Hope walked toward Rachael, rubbing her arms as if she were cold. Rachael reached out for Hope's hand, probably in an attempt to take her out of the rain.

"You're it!" Hope yelled as she slapped Rachael's hand and ran away.

Everyone, including Joe, quickly ran away from Rachael.

"So, we're gonna play like that," Rachael called after them.

Soon, the chase was underway. All the kids and a good number of adults joined the game. They were running and splashing in the streets while the rain fell around them and the thunder boomed overhead.

"You know you're crazy, right?" Shawn laughed as he pulled her close.

"It's part of the reason you love me," Emily smiled at him.

"Damn straight," Shawn nodded as he pulled her into a kiss.

They played for a bit longer, but the lightning grew brighter in the sky. It was time to get out of the rain. She walked inside with Shawn, Hope, and Marley. They dripped water through the house and went to warm showers and dry clothes. She made them a quick supper as they were all tired from the game and eager for bed.

"I pulled everyone off the wall tonight," Shawn told her as they climbed into bed. "Seemed like too much of a risk."

"I agree," Emily nodded. "I'm sure we will be fine until the storm passes.

"What came over you tonight?" Shawn asked, pulling her close. "Don't get me wrong, I love seeing you like that."

"I don't know," Emily admitted. "Just something in that moment, I felt free. No responsibilities, no worries. I was just free."

"If there's anything I can do to make that happen more often, just let me know," Shawn replied, squeezing her tight.

She lay beside Shawn, listening to the rain fall outside the window. The storm was getting worse outside, but that didn't matter. It didn't take long for her to fall asleep.

The following day, she discovered that Shawn had already gotten up. The storm was still raging outside and seemed worse than the night before. She got up and quickly dressed. She made her way downstairs just as Shawn came through the front door.

"How is it out there?" Emily asked.

"It's getting pretty rough," Shawn said, shaking off some of the rainwater. "I think it may be best if everyone stays home today." "That bad?" Emily asked.

"I don't want anyone on the wall," Shawn replied. "I climbed up and nearly broke my neck. There's so much rainwater that we now have a mote forming around the wall."

"Shit," Emily gasped. "How loud is it out there?"

Shawn looked at her, confused, and did not respond.

"Do you think everyone would hear me if I made an announcement over the speakers?" Emily explained. "It would be faster than going door to door."

"Sarah's got those things so loud that if it wasn't for the wall, you could hear them two states over," Shawn replied.

She nodded as she grabbed her walkie.

"Attention," She said after turning the walkie to the correct channel. "Due to the storm, everyone needs to stay home. Wall duty and all other jobs are suspended at this time. Please reach out if you need anything to help you get through this."

She quickly flipped the walkie back to the group station just as Jacob began to speak.

"We are good out here for today," Jacob said. "If this lasts more than a few days, though, we may need some help."

"You can let everyone know I'll still be in the store," Jessica said next. "If they can't get to me, I'll bring them what they need."

She waited while each council member checked in, telling her what they would be doing. None of them would take a day off. Once everyone had reported in, she turned the walkie back to the speaker channel. She informed everyone that the store would still be open for essentials only, and Jessica would deliver if they couldn't make it. Sarah would be providing each house with an emergency walkie to help with communication, which would need to be returned after the storm.

"That went pretty smoothly," Shawn smiled as she sat down on the couch.

"It's just started," Emily smiled back at him. "I'm sure there will be a hiccup somewhere."

"No sense in worrying about that now," Shawn replied, walking towards the kitchen. "Why don't you get Hope up, and I'll start on breakfast?"

She knew he was trying to distract her from her worry, so she decided to let him. She stood back up and made her way up the stairs. Hope was still asleep, but Marley looked at her as she opened the door.

"Time to get up," Emily grinned as she walked in.

"But it's still nighttime," Hope said, looking out the window.

"No," Emily assured her. "The storms are just blocking the sun today.

"Did I miss school?!" Hope asked, jumping out of bed.

"There's no school today," Emily said, trying to calm her. "Or work. Everyone is going to stay home until the storm is over."

"Can we play a game?" Hope asked with a smile.

"Only if you get dressed and your chores are done," Emily laughed. "Daddy has already started breakfast.

Hope petted Marley on the head as she quickly picked out her clothes and began to dress. Emily headed back downstairs, and moments later, Hope ran past her. Marley hesitated only a moment at the back door, not wanting to go out in the storm. However, his urge to go to the bathroom was too strong, and he ran outside. Hope was still filling his food when Marley came running back through the door, soaking wet.

"Maybe next time we should cover him in soap, so he smells better when he comes in," Emily teased.

Marley was too hungry to be insulted and quickly began to eat his breakfast. Emily, Shawn, and Hope ate breakfast slowly this morning. They decided to take their time with nothing pulling them out of the house. Once breakfast was done and cleaned up, they were all set to do the household chores they usually wouldn't be able to do. Hope confirmed several times that they could play some games once they were done. Both Emily and Shawn agreed they would once the work was done.

It was after lunch that Hope got to set up the first game, Monopoly. They had just set up everything on the table when the walkie suddenly came to life.

"Emily," Jessica's voice rang out.

"I'm here," Emily replied after picking up the walkie. "Everything okay?"

"No," Jessica quickly replied. "I'm sorry to ask, but can you come to the store?"

"I prefer if you didn't," Shawn quickly said. "It's still really nasty out there."

"Is it something that I can maybe talk you through?" Emily asked Jessica.

"Is Hope near you?" Jessica asked.

She looked at Hope, who seemed confused by the question. She understood, though. This had something to do with Chad or Veronica.

"She is," Emily answered. "I'll be there in just a minute."

"Do you really have to go?" Hope pouted in her seat.

"Just for a minute," Emily assured her. "Make sure Daddy doesn't steal any extra money, and I'll be right back."

"You need me to go with you?" Shawn asked.

She could tell by the look on his face that he figured out the same thing she did.

"I got it," Emily assured him. "I'll just be gone a few minutes."

"Take Marley and radio if you need me," Shawn said as he kissed her.

"Yes, sir," Emily smiled as she turned to leave.

Marley stood with her by the door and looked at her like she was crazy when she opened it.

"You're not scared of a little rain, are you?" Emily teased as she walked out.

Marley seemed to understand as he followed her. She and Marley made their way across the street to the store, each soaked when they walked in.

"I'll need a boat if this gets much worse," Emily teased as she looked at Jessica.

"We have a big problem," Jessica replied quickly.

She couldn't help but be a little taken aback. No matter how serious the situation, Jessica always welcomed her small talk.

"What's going on?" Emily asked after looking around the store and seeing no one else.

"I've been having Veronica work the back room mostly," Jessica began. "As usual, she didn't stock before she left yesterday, so I was doing it today."

"Okay," Emily nodded, confused. She knew that there had to be more than just this for Jessica to call her here.

"We have quite a bit of missing inventory," Jessica continued.

"So, we will just dock her credits. She's just pocketing what she wants," Emily nodded.

"It's more than that," Jessica continued. "The amount that's missing is more than three could eat."

"How much?" Emily asked.

"Honestly, enough to feed an army," Jessica stated. "I found this stuffed into a pallet." Jessica handed Emily a piece of paper. She looked down at it and read the list that was written.

2 sacks of grain

5 sacks of flour
12 dozen eggs
AS Toilet paper
5 cases of MREs
AS Vitamins
AS Medical supplies
AS Socks
AS Meat/Protein

"Is this a shopping list?" Emily asked, looking over the paper.

"There's a stack of most of the stuff back there," Jessica explained. "It looks like the storm interrupted her shopping spree."

"What the hell is she going to do with all of this?" Emily asked, confused.

"Turn it over," Jessica instructed her.

She turned over the paper in her hands and could feel the color drain from her face as she read.

½ remaining ammo
½ remaining explosives
½ gun supply
Maps of Sanctuary
Patrol schedule

"What the fuck?!" Emily said, looking back at Jessica. "They don't have access to the armory!"

"Apparently, she thinks she found a way in," Jessica remarked. "The stack back there already includes the maps and patrol schedule.

"And the rest?" Emily asked with a lump in her throat.

"Not back there, but I can't know for sure," Jessica said slowly.

"Put it all back on the shelves," Emily said after a few minutes. "I'll take the maps and the schedule."

"What are you going to do?" Jessica asked, handing them over.

"Figure out what they wanted them for," Emily said confidently. "I'll go with Shawn tonight and inventory the armory. If anything's missing, we'll arrest them both. If not, I think it's time to change the game."

"I don't understand," Jessica replied.

"She's not going to be working here anymore," Emily grinned. "After the storm, she will report directly to me.

"Is that a good idea?" Jessica asked with concern. "Giving her more access to this place may not be the best move."

"Keeping her where I can see her is," Emily replied. "Let's keep this to ourselves for now."

"You're the boss," Jessica said. "My lips are sealed.

She turned and left the store with Marley. They quickly ran home, but she did not find the same comfort inside as she did when she left.

"Everything alright?" Shawn asked as she walked in.

"Under control," Emily smiled as she sat down. "I'll explain later."

"Are we ready to play?" Hope asked.

"Let's do it," Emily replied, handing Hope the dice.

Shawn kept eyeing her for the rest of the day, trying to get some clues as to what was happening. Once Hope was in bed, Shawn waited for her to explain.

"Jessica found some suspicious stuff at the store," Emily began. "We need to go do an inventory of the armory."

"How bad is it?" Shawn asked, walking towards the door.

"I won't know that until after the inventory," Emily admitted.

She and Shawn spent hours in the armory, checking that all weapons and ammo were accounted for. She couldn't help but sigh with relief that nothing was missing.

"They need to leave," Shawn said without hesitation.

"That may just put us at more risk," Emily explained. "They know a lot about how we work, what we have, and who is here. I think it's best to keep them here and figure out why they were gathering this stuff."

"It's too risky," Shawn insisted.

"It's the least risky option," Emily said. "That much stuff couldn't have just been for them. Either other people inside are working with them or...."

"They have people outside the wall," Shawn finished for her.

"Either way," Emily continued. "Kicking them out puts us at risk."

"I'll ensure I'm here whenever weapons come in or out," Shawn said. "But what are we going to do about the store?"

"I'm going to reassign her," Emily replied.

"Where?" Shawn almost laughed. "She has almost no skills."

"As my personal assistant," Emily said quickly. "She will feel like she hit the jackpot, and I will get to keep a close eye on her."

"There are so many ways this could go wrong," Shawn said, shaking his head.

"Do you have a better idea?" Emily asked.

Shawn stood in silence.

"Then it's settled. Let's go home."

Chapter 4

The storm continued for two more days. The tension in the house from Jessica's discovery was heavy. Shawn was still unhappy about Emily's decision and did not attempt to hide it. Emily practically burst out the door on Saturday morning, the first clear day.

Shawn had already left for work, and Hope was at Rachael's for the day with Marley. Emily quickly made her way through town, surveying the storm's damage. A walk around the wall would give her a general overview of things. She walked her way up the wall and looked over things, both inside and out. Several trees were down, and there were some areas where the water had pooled up. She couldn't see them, but she was sure the zombie pits were flooded.

"Looks like things held up pretty good," Emily said.

She turned back down the stairs just as Chad reached the top. She was determined not to speak to him and attempted to walk past.

"Emily," Chad said, standing in her way. "I really need to talk to you."

"I have work to do," Emily replied shortly.

"You can take a few minutes," Chad insisted, still blocking her path. "It's about Hope."

"She's with Rachael today, but I'll let you know when and if she wants to see you again," Emily said coldly, still trying to push her way past him.

"Damn it!" Chad yelled, still not letting her pass. "I want her to come live with me for a while."

"Excuse me?" Emily replied, shocked. "Why the hell would I agree to that?!"

"I'm not asking you," Chad spat back at her. "I wanted to move in with you, give our family a chance. But you refuse to do the right thing."

"You think you can just take her?!" Emily yelled back, shaking with anger.

"We've talked about it," Chad smiled at her in his evil way. "Veronica always wanted a daughter. We can give her someone other than a dog to play with. Unless you reconsider my offer from yesterday?"

"You really think you can blackmail me?!" Emily yelled, getting closer to Chad. "I will have to be permanently dead before my daughter ever lives with you!"

She managed to finally push past Chad and to the stairs.

"Stay the fuck away from my daughter and me!" Emily spat at him as she took her first step.

She felt the pressure of Chad touching her back and then lost the feeling of everything around her. The stairs disappeared under her feet, and Chad's hand disappeared from her back. Everything felt like it was moving in slow motion. She desperately tried to grab onto something to stop herself. But the stairs were quickly approaching, and her hands found nothing.

She wrapped her arms around her lower stomach and attempted to shield the baby from the impact as best she could. She collided with the first step hard. The pain radiated through her arm and shoulder. She didn't have time to cry out before the subsequent collision, this time to her head.

She tried to focus on her arms, keeping them in place to protect the baby. However, her vision blurred, and she could feel her arms slipping away. She felt everything going dark around her as the collision continued. She couldn't help but feel relief as she landed on the ground. The pain was horrific, but at least it wouldn't get any worse.

"Mommy!" Hopes scream wrang out.

She tried to will herself to speak and tell Hope she was okay. But she couldn't will herself to do it.

"What happened?" Cole's voice rang out next to her.

"She fell," Hope sobbed.

"Your mama's gonna be fine," Cole said in his most soothing voice. However, she could feel the worry behind his words. "Doc, Shawn, get to the wall immediately," Cole said calmly into the radio.

Emily didn't hear a response and assumed they were just each making their way to her.

"She's bleeding," Hope cried.

"I know, sweetie," Cole comforted her. "Doc will get her all fixed up.

Emily could feel the warmth of the blood running on her face. But that wasn't what made her want to cry. Her lower stomach hurt, and she could feel the warm blood between her legs. She knew something was happening to the baby.

"What happened?!" Doc yelled as he reached them.

"She fell down the stairs," Cole explained. "I think from the top."

"Her arms broken," Doc said, focusing on her. "And she's definitely got at least a concussion. We need to get her to the clinic; she should be fine to move."

"Emily!" Shawn yelled with pain in his voice.

"We need to get her to the clinic," Doc repeated.

As Shawn picked her up, she wanted to scream in pain, but no noise came.

"Stay with Aunt Rachael," Shawn
instructed Hope as he carried her inside.

"Put her here," Doc told Shawn.

She felt Shawn place her down as gently
as he could, but the pain still radiated
throughout her body.

"We need to set her arm and stitch her
forehead," Doc said more to himself than
Shawn.

"What can I do?" Shawn asked.

She could tell he was holding back tears.
She wanted to comfort him and tell him she was
fine, but the darkness started taking over her
mind. In part, she was grateful for a break from
the pain, but hated to leave him alone at that
moment.

Emily slowly opened her eyes in the quiet
room of the clinic. Shawn sat by her bedside,
asleep but holding her hand. She lay still, the
pain slowly creeping back in. However, she
didn't make a sound. She didn't want to wake
Shawn. She was sure he never left her side and
had to be exhausted. She lay still for several
minutes until Doc came through the door.

"I'm glad to see you awake," Doc smiled
at her. "You took a pretty nasty fall."

"Not by choice," Emily grimaced in pain.

"What do you mean?" Shawn asked
beside her.

"I was trying to let you sleep," Emily
forced herself to smile at him.

"I'm fine," Shawn assured her. "Emily, what happened?

Hope saw the whole thing, but she won't talk about it. Every time we try, she starts crying and hides her face in Marley's fur."

"She saw," Emily felt more pain from that statement than she did from the fall.

"Emily," Shawn said, squeezing her hand. "What happened?"

"The baby?" Emily asked, choking back tears.

She already knew the answer in her heart, but still had to ask.

"I'm sorry," Doc said slowly. "I can repair broken arms and stitch cuts, but I couldn't...."

She felt the hot tears run down her face. The baby was gone, stolen by Chad. She could feel rage, but the pain of losing the baby was stronger.

"It's okay, babe," Shawn said as he stood and held her.

She felt herself thinking back to when she lost the baby with Chad. It was when their relationship soured and she lost the man she once loved. Chad had told her the same thing, and things still went wrong. Hearing Shawn's words, remembering her past, she felt no comfort in his touch.

"I'm sorry," Emily cried.

"You have nothing to be sorry for," Shawn assured her.

"You say that now, but I know how this works," Emily continued to cry.

Shawn pulled back and looked confused. She watched, still crying, as he finally realized what she was talking about.

"I'm not him," Shawn said, caressing her face. "I love you no matter what. We will get through this."

"No, we won't," Emily sobbed.

"Yes, we will," Shawn assured her.

Shawn held her and allowed her to cry for several more minutes. Once her tears had slowed, Shawn returned to sitting in his chair and holding her hand.

"Emily," Shawn began. "What happened?"

"I was arguing with Chad," Emily said, still crying. "He said he would take Hope, and I told him over my dead body. Then I started on my way down the stairs."

She started crying again, unable to finish her story.

"He pushed you," Shawn said firmly.

"I tried to protect the baby, but when I hit my head, I couldn't anymore," She cried.

"This isn't your fault," Shawn insisted. "It's his."

Emily could hear the anger in his voice. His grip on her hand tightened.

"Shawn?" Emily said, still crying.

"I'm going to kill him," Shawn said, standing up.

"No!" Emily heard herself yell.

"Emily," Shawn replied, trying not to yell.

"You can't kill him," Emily said. "We need to know what they are up to."

"I'll torture it out of him," Shawn said coldly.

"We can't," Emily sobbed. "You can't."

"It's not something that should be handled right now anyway," Doc spoke. "Right now, we need to focus on Emily and helping Hope deal with the trauma she saw."

She watched as Shawn forced himself to push his anger down. She knew it wouldn't last long, but he would now put away his blood thirst.

"You are going to need to rest," Doc said to Emily. "You will be in that cast for at least six weeks."

She looked down at her right arm to see that it was in a plaster cast.

"The stitches can come out in a few weeks," Doc continued. "It was a pretty nasty gash. The other bumps and bruises will heal independently over the next few weeks."

"Can I take her home?" Shawn asked, breaking his silence.

"Of course," Doc nodded. "But rest until I say otherwise."

"I can do that," Emily nodded, still crying.

"Where's Hope?" Emily asked, looking at Shawn.

"She's with your family," Shawn replied. "Chad has been trying to see her, but she refuses. Now I understand why."

"Shawn," Emily cried, reaching for his hand.

"I'm here," Shawn smiled down at her. "Let's get you and our daughter home."

"Okay," Emily nodded.

"Here's her medication," Doc said, handing a bottle to Shawn. "I've written down her pill schedule."

"Got it," Shawn nodded. "Let's get going, babe."

She held onto him as she slowly stood up. She knew the rage was still inside him, but he hid it. She knew it wasn't healthy, but right now, she didn't care. She wanted to keep him for as long as she could. Shawn wrapped his arm around her and walked her out of the clinic.

"You sure you're okay to walk?" Shawn asked once they were outside.

"Holding on to you, I can do anything," Emily forced herself to smile at him.

"I've got you," Shawn assured her as they started walking again.

She walked slowly with Shawn into the house and lay on the couch. She knew she wasn't ready for the stairs, and Shawn seemed to know the same thing.

"I'll be back," Shawn said once she was settled.

"Where are you going?" Emily asked with panic.

"Just to pick up Hope and let your family know you are awake," Shawn assured her. "I'll ask them to give you two sometime before visiting."

"Alright," Emily replied, tears streaming down her face.

"Just rest," Shawn said as he kissed her lightly. "I'll be home soon."

She lay her head back as Shawn walked out the door. The tears were flowing freely at this point. She knew that she needed to get it to stop before Hope got home. She forced herself to push her emotions down, and the tears slowly stopped. She had regained her composure just as the front door opened.

"Mommy!" Hope yelled as she ran into the living room.

"Right here," Emily smiled at her.

Hope ran to Emily and wrapped her arms around her. She didn't care about the pain as she hugged Hope back.

"I'm fine," Emily assured her.

"I thought…" Hope began as she started crying.

"Never," Emily smiled at her. "Your mom's pretty tough."

"I love you, Mommy," Hope said, tightening her hug.

"I love you too, baby," Emily said softly. She held Hope for what seemed forever. Slowly, she pulled Hope down next to her on the couch.

"Daddy says you saw what happened," Emily said to Hope. "But that you won't talk about it."

"I didn't want to lose daddy, too," Hope cried. "I knew that he would be angry."

"It's our job to protect you," Emily said softly to Hope. "Daddy can't do his job if you don't talk to him. You have to trust Daddy."

"I do," Hope said with tears in her eyes, looking at Shawn. "I'm sorry, daddy."

"I understand," Shawn said, sitting on the coffee table.

"I'm ready to talk about it," Hope said as she stood up and crawled into Shawn's lap.

"Are you sure?" Shawn said, helping her up.

"Mommy and Chad looked like they were fighting," Hope said, looking at her hands. "I heard mommy yell over my dead body."

"It's okay," Shawn assured her as Hope paused.

"Mommy started down the stairs, and Chad pushed her," Hope said, crying. "I watched mommy fall, and he just stood there."

Hope buried her face in her hands and cried. Shawn wrapped his arms around her and held her.

"It's okay," Shawn said. "No one is going to hurt mommy anymore."

"He tried to kill her," Hope cried. "I thought he had."

"Look," Shawn said, pulling Hope's hands from her face. "She's right there."

Hope smiled at her, her face stained with tears.

"If there's anything I've learned about Mom, it's that she is not going to die so easily," Shawn smiled at Hope. "The stubborn ones are like that."

"She is pretty stubborn," Hope smiled.

"That tells me that she is going to be around a long time," Shawn said with a smile.

"Are we kicking Chad out?" Hope asked.

"Well," Emily began.

"I think we should," Hope interrupted. "We don't need evil people here."

"I agree," Emily nodded. "But we are not kicking him out."

"Why?!" Hope asked, visibly angry.

"It's hard to explain," Emily began. "I need you to trust that this is best for now."

"What if he tries again?" Hope cried.

"We won't give him a chance," Shawn spoke. "Mommy will never be alone, so where can he get to her?"

"How can we be sure?" Hope asked Shawn.

"I promise," Shawn assured her. "I would never break a promise to you, would I?"

"No," Hope replied slowly. "But can we keep him away from me, too? I don't want to see him anymore."

"If that's your decision," Emily said. "I don't want you making it because you think it's what we want."

"It's what I want," Hope said astutely. "I don't want anyone in my life who wants to hurt my family."

"Speaking of family," Emily said, looking around. "Where's Marley?"

"Grandma's going to bring him when they come for dinner," Hope explained. "He's been really upset these past few days."

"Days?!" Emily asked in shock. "I was out for days?"

"Yeah," Shawn nodded. "That's why we were so worried."

"I'm so sorry," Emily said to Hope and Shawn.

"Just no more long naps," Hope smiled. "You can just sleep more at night."

"Deal," Emily laughed. "I'd better get started on dinner."

"No!" Hope and Shawn yelled at the same time.

She froze in her spot on the couch.

"You just lay there," Shawn smiled as they stood up. "We'll take care of dinner."

She lay on the couch while Hope and Shawn took off for the kitchen. She listened to them work, and it wasn't long before Shawn appeared with her pills and a glass of water. She took her medicine without complaint, and Shawn returned to the kitchen. It wasn't much longer, and the front door opened. She knew that it was her family arriving to check on her.

"Hello," Emily called out.

Instantly, she heard nails scraping on the hardwood floors. She watched as Marley ran towards her at full speed, stopping just before her. Marley rested his head on her lap, and she began to pet him.

"We were beginning to worry something was wrong with him," Christine said as she walked in. "How are you feeling, sweetie?"

"Like I fell off the wall," Emily teased.

"I meant about the miscarriage," Christine confirmed.

She looked at her, confused.

"Shawn told us," Christine told her. "I don't think he meant to. It just slipped out."

"Sorry, we hadn't told you yet," Emily said with shame in her voice.

"It was a secret for the two of you to keep until you were ready," Christine assured her. "I just want you to understand that we are here for you, and so is he."

"I'm afraid this will get worse before it gets better," Emily said with tears in her eyes.

"It may," Christine said in a soothing voice. "But I know you and him will come out strong on the other side."

"I'm scared," Emily confessed.

"There's no reason to be," Rachael said, stepping forward. "You are the strongest person we know."

"There's no way you've been through all of this not to come out better on the other side," Charlie said next.

"One question," Joe asked. "Is Chad really off-limits?"

"For now," Emily nodded. "I can't explain why, but…."

"Then don't," Joe smiled. "I trust you. We all do. So, if you say off-limits for now, that's how it is."

"But can we please get Veronica back to work?" Rachael sighed. "She has begun to terrorize the village."

"Yeah," Emily laughed. "First thing tomorrow."

Chapter 5

She had Veronica report to her early the following day, after Hope was at school. Veronica was displeased to learn she had a new job, but quickly got over it when she realized she was her assistant. Veronica made nasty comments about other people in Sanctuary and how things were being run, but nothing Emily couldn't tolerate.

Shawn couldn't stand to be in the house while Veronica was there. Emily knew that he hated Veronica just as much as he did Chad. He agreed to wait to give Chad what he deserved. But that didn't mean he was going to play nice. She accepted that but knew that she had a job to do.

Emily kept Veronica busy delivering notes around town and making her lunch. Veronica kept asking when she would get more serious work. Emily kept saying they were limited in what they could do now, with her stuck on the couch. Veronica was not happy with the answer, but she accepted it.

Emily had hoped after a few weeks to notice something to give her a clue as to what Veronica was up to, but the weeks passed, and there was still nothing.

"She's good at hiding what she's up to," Emily confessed to Shawn as they lay in bed. "I'm unsure what to do to make her slip up."

"They are being extra cautious after the fall," Shawn replied. "They will be that way until they think they are clear."

"I've been telling everyone that I slipped," Emily said. "Only you and my family know the truth."

"I think that's what they are afraid of," Shawn sighed. "We will have to do something to make them think otherwise."

"Like what?" Emily asked, having no idea what he was thinking.

"You trust me, right?" Shawn asked.

"Of course," Emily replied.

"I want to get this over with fast, and I don't see any other way," Shawn said.

"What are you talking about?" Emily asked, looking at him.

"We break up publicly. I move out, and we make them think at least part of their plan is working," Shawn replied.

"We what?!" Emily asked. "I'm not giving you up to figure this out."

"You're not, Shawn said, taking her hand. "It will all just be an act."

"How do we explain that to Hope?" Emily asked.

"We don't," Shawn answered if it was apparent. "No one can know except for you and me."

"We can't do that to her," Emily said. "We can't put her through that."

"We have to," Shawn said softly. "It's the only way we can get this over with and ensure she is safe."

"I don't know if I can do it," Emily admitted, trying not to cry.

"You can," Shawn assured her. "It will kill me, but knowing it will make you safe in the long run is worth it."

"I just don't know," Emily said, looking up at the ceiling.

"We have to do this," Shawn said. "As much as we love each other, I know we can do it."

"How do we do this?" Emily said with a sigh.

She and Shawn lay in bed for the next few hours plotting their fake breakup for the next day. They talked out every detail to sell the story, including fights they would have after Shawn moved out. When they finished, Shawn simply held her in his arms.

"I love you," Shawn whispered to her.

"I love you too," Emily whispered back.

"As long as we both know that, we are going to be fine," Shawn said as he kissed her.

"I don't know how I'm going to sleep without you," Emily said as she snuggled closer.

"It's just for a little while," Shawn assured her. "Then you will never have to let me go again."

"I'll hold you to that," Emily replied.

"Please do," Shawn grinned at her.

She tried her best to stay awake, to soak in every moment she could with Shawn. But sleep overtook her at some point. Shawn woke her early the following day for them to begin the morning routine. She didn't want to get out of bed. She was not ready for them to put their plan into action.

She and Shawn quickly worked their way through the morning. Shawn broke from the plan a little in saying goodbye to Hope. Shawn held her in a long hug and told her to remember that he loved her, now and always. Hope didn't think much of it and told Shawn she loved him, too.

Emily watched as Shawn walked out the door with Hope. Her heart broke a little, knowing that this was the last time her family would be together for a while. Veronica showed up a few minutes later, ready to get to work. She was supposed to go to the clinic today for a check-up on her arm. This was the plan, where the breakup would start to take shape.

Veronica sat impatiently in the waiting room while she went back. Doc looked her over and seemed pleased with how she was healing.

"A few more weeks in the cast, and you will be as good as new," he remarked.

"I don't know about that," Emily replied. "Nothing will be the same."

"You're young," Doc assured her. "You and Shawn will be able to try again."

"I'm not sure I want to," Emily replied.

"Emily," Doc said, looking at her with concern. "Is everything alright?"

"It's fine," Emily said, wiping the tears from her eyes. "So, I'm officially off bed rest?"

"Yes," Doc replied slowly. "But I still want you to take it slow."

"Thanks, Doc," Emily said as she stood up and left the room.

She had done her part, planted the first seed about trouble in paradise. She felt terrible about having to deceive her most trusted friends, but they had no choice.

"Let's go," Emily said to Veronica as she walked through the waiting room.

"To the office?" Veronica asked, standing up.

"I need to check in around town first," Emily replied flatly.

"Is everything alright?" Veronica asked with a surprising amount of concern.

"No," Emily replied shortly.

She didn't stop as she walked out of the clinic. Veronica didn't ask any more questions but simply followed her around town. Everyone seemed to notice that her behavior was different, but no one questioned her. No one except for Sarah.

"What is with you and Shawn today?" Sarah asked without hesitation. "You both are extra grumpy."

"It's really none of your business," Emily snapped back.

"I don't know who you think you're talking to, but…." Sarah began angrily.

She didn't wait for her to finish and instead stormed out of the COM building. She caught Chad looking at Veronica, who was smiling. The plan was working, but she knew that she owed Sarah one hell of an apology when it was over.

"You've done good," Emily said to Veronica. "Everything seems to be in order."

"I hope you are willing to trust me with more now," Veronica smiled at her.

"Yeah," Emily nodded. "I'll show you how to work the inventory reports later."

"I can handle that," Veronica nodded. "And anything else you want help with."

"Good," Emily nodded. "I might need more from you than I thought."

"I am here to help," Veronica smiled.

She said nothing and instead headed to her office. She walked behind the desk and grabbed the inventory reports. She handed them to Veronica and showed her how to update the reports. Veronica took to it quickly and worked while she rested on the couch.

"What is she doing!?" Shawn yelled, coming into the office.

"Working!" Emily yelled back at him.

"You are really going to let this crazy bitch handle this?!" Shawn yelled.

"She's my assistant!" Emily yelled back. "She assists with whatever I need!"

"We agreed that she would deliver notes and fetch your coffee!" Shawn continued to yell.

"You ordered; I didn't agree!" Emily yelled back.

"Fine!" Shawn yelled back. "Do whatever the fuck you want!"

With that, Shawn stormed out of the office. Emily knew everything he was going to say, but it didn't keep it from hurting. Veronica had stopped working and was watching the scene unfold. Emily could not allow her emotions to take over. She had to continue with the plan. She quickly stood up and followed Shawn onto the street, Veronica behind her.

"What is your problem?!" Emily yelled at Shawn once they reached the street.

"You are!" Shawn yelled, turning back to face her. "Ever since he arrived, you've been pushing me away."

"Ever since he arrived, you seem to think you're in charge!" Emily yelled back.

"You know what," Shawn practically growled at her. "He was right. You need to be with him!"

"You're still telling me what to do!" Emily yelled back at him.

"You won't have to worry about that anymore!" Shawn said with all the hate he could muster.

"You're right!" Emily yelled back. "Get your crap out of my house and stay away from me!"

"No problem!" Shawn yelled back as he stormed away.

"And stay the hell away from my daughter!" Emily yelled at him.

Shawn didn't say a word but flipped her off as he walked away. Emily had seen him act cold towards her before, with Jeff. But this was ten times worse than she could have even imagined. She had come to count on Shawn as a protector. And for the time being, she had to face things without him.

"I guess this means the wedding is off," Veronica mused behind her.

"Don't you have work to do?" Emily turned on Veronica.

"Yes, ma'am," Veronica replied as she turned and headed back inside.

"Emily?" Joe spoke up behind her.

"Not now," Emily replied as she wiped the tears from her face and stormed back inside.

The tears were not part of the plan. They were honest, and she didn't try to hide them. She sat at the council table, Marley lying at her feet. He seemed more confused than anything about the situation. Yet, he still wanted to try and comfort her.

Hours passed, and she finally ran out of tears to cry. She was staring at the table when Veronica came out of the office.

"The reports are done," Veronica said. "Is there anything else you need?"

"You can go," Emily said flatly.

"I'm supposed to stay until at least three," Veronica replied.

"I'm done for the day," Emily said snappily. "I want to be alone."

"Do you need me and Chad to pick up Hope?" Veronica asked.

"No," Emily quickly replied. "I've got it."

Veronica nodded and walked out of the building. Emily could tell by her wicked smile that the plan was working. But that did not help the pain she felt in her heart. She sat with Marley until it was time to pick up Hope. She was sure that Shawn had his stuff out of the house by now, and it was time to break another heart. She made her way to the school and forced herself to smile as Hope ran toward her.

"I made Daddy a present today," Hope said, holding up a painting.

"That's nice," Emily smiled. "But you will not see Shawn for a while."

"Why not?" Hope asked, concerned. "Did he get hurt?"

"No," Emily assured her. "He's fine. We'll talk about it at home."

Hope was confused but took her hand as they headed home. She could tell the difference as they walked up to the house. The motorcycle was gone, and Hope noticed right away.

"Did Daddy go outside the wall?" Hope asked.

"No," Emily said as softly as she could. She opened the door and led Hope and Marley inside. The house felt empty inside. It was like a piece was missing.

"Mommy, what's going on?" Hope asked once they were inside.

"Shawn and I aren't getting married anymore," Emily explained.

"Why not?" Hope asked, holding back tears.

"He's not my happily ever after," Emily said, trying not to cry. "I guess I will have to keep looking."

"But you and daddy are forever," Hope said, confused, tears running down her cheeks. "We're not," Emily said, trying to stay strong. "He's returned to the apartments, and we will not see him for a while."

"But I can still see him, right?" Hope asked, crying.

"Not right now," Emily answered. "I know this hurts, but I need you to understand that I must keep my life separate from his. Otherwise, I can't move on."

"It's just a fight," Hope insisted. "You don't need to move on. You and Daddy just need to say you're sorry."

"But we're not," Emily said. "I'm sorry,

Hope. This is not something that can be fixed."

She resisted every urge to scoop up Hope and tell her it was all an act. Hope stood crying, not understanding what had happened.

"I'm sorry, sweetie," Emily said, pulling Hope into a hug.

"But we'll be okay, just you and me."

"Can I go to my room?" Hope asked, still crying.

"If you want," Emily replied.

Hope pulled away from her and ran up to her room in tears. Emily knew that this was cruel, but had no choice. She could only pray that Hope would understand when this was all over. She nodded towards the staircase, and Marley took off to be with Hope. She made the two of them supper, but Hope barely ate a bite. After an hour of staring at her plate, she asked to return to her room once more. Emily allowed her to go while she cleaned up dinner. She went into Hope's room to tuck her in and found Hope crying on her bed.

"Sweetie," Emily said as she walked into the room and sat next to Hope. "I know it hurts, and you don't understand."

"Why did this happen?" Hope asked.

This was Hope's first time talking since she told her that she and Shawn had broken up.

"These things happen sometimes," Emily replied as tears welled up in her eyes. "It hurts me too."

This was the first honest thing she had been able to say to Hope since the act started.

"I'm sorry, mommy," Hope said as she climbed into her lap.

"I don't want you to hate him," Emily said.

She knew she was going off script, but couldn't let Hope suffer this way.

"I need it to be the two of us for a while."

"I can do that," Hope nodded. "Everything will work out if it's meant to be."

"But if it's not," Emily began. "We will still be okay."

"As long as you and I are together," Hope finished for her.

"That's right," Emily smiled through her tears.

"Can Marley and I sleep in your room tonight?" Hope asked.

"Of course," Emily smiled. "I don't think I can sleep alone."

"You don't have to, mommy," Hope said as she hugged her. "You got me."

"And I thank God for that every day," Emily said as she hugged Hope back.

She helped Hope gather a few things before they went to her room. Hope crawled up on the bed and lay down with Marley at her feet. She turned off the light and crawled in beside her. Hope slowly fell asleep. Emily lay in the dark and watched her. She knew that Hope was hurting, but was glad that somehow, she had brought some comfort to her. She waited until she was sure Hope was sound asleep before she let her own emotions out. She stayed silent as she allowed the tears to flow freely. It may have been an act, but it still hurt like hell. She eventually cried herself to sleep just before dawn.

Hope woke her the following day, much later than they should have gotten up. She forced herself through the morning routine and dropped Hope off at school late.

Hope hugged her and told her she loved her before heading to school. She turned with Marley and headed up to meet Veronica for work. Her skin crawled at the thought of seeing Veronica now, but she knew she had no choice. Veronica stood waiting in front of the town hall. She gathered herself and stood tall as she approached.

"Good morning," Veronica smiled at her as she neared.

"Good morning," Emily answered. "You ready to get to work?"

"Of course," Veronica smiled.

"Then let's get going," Emily said as she turned and started her morning check-ins.

Everyone kept things short and to the point, sensing that she was not ready to talk about yesterday. She was thankful for that. She wasn't prepared to move into that stage of the plan. She checked in with Sam, who seemed even more awkward than everyone else.

Everything seemed as it should be, and she wasn't sure why he seemed so nervous.

"Shawn gave me his reports," Sam said as she turned to leave.

"He did?" Emily asked as she turned back.

"He said it would be best if I gave them to you," Sam said, holding out the papers.

"Thanks," Emily said, taking them from him and then turning to leave.

"The coward couldn't even do his job," Veronica said as they walked out the door.

"Doesn't surprise me," Emily said as coldly as she could.

"If he can't face you to give a report, how can you trust him to be the head of your security?" Veronica asked.

It may have sounded like a simple question to an outsider, but she knew Veronica was working an angle.

"You're right," Emily replied. "But it will have to wait. If I do it now, everyone will assume I fired him because of the breakup."

"Of course," Veronica agreed. "It's best to wait an appropriate amount of time."

Emily began to lead Veronica and Marley back to the town hall. Shawn was walking towards them up the street. She resisted everything in her that wanted to run to him. This was the plan, their way of reminding each other that it was all an act. Shawn crossed to the other side of the street, pulling at the front of his vest,

and she tucked her hair behind her ears.
Uncomfortable gestures to anyone looking, their
new way of saying "I love you," until the
mystery was solved.

Chapter 6

The weeks crawled, and Emily couldn't wait until the rouse she and Shawn were doing was over. They had continued their subtle gestures each time they saw each other. Everyone in Sanctuary was avoiding the topic of the breakup except for Veronica. She talked about it every chance she got, making Emily sick to her stomach to play along. However, Veronica didn't seem to notice.

Everyone else in Sanctuary made every effort not to discuss the breakup. Whenever the subject did come up, they quickly and awkwardly changed the subject. Everyone who was, except for Emily's family. Her siblings, in particular, were unwilling to accept the story and questioned her every chance they got. She tried her best to excuse herself from these conversations, knowing they would be able to talk the truth out of her. This only seemed to confirm to them that something wasn't right.

Two months had passed, the wedding date had passed, and Emily felt that she was no closer to learning anything about what Veronica was up to. Mostly, Veronica talked about things that meant nothing. Things such as putting in coffee shops and high-end clothing stores, and changing the currency system. She also thought those in higher-up positions should earn more than general labor. Emily knew Veronica was only saying these things out of selfish aspirations, but had to play her part. She had become accustomed to faking enthusiasm about each suggestion and telling her they would need to wait for the right time to implement them.

Veronica was also pushing Hope to resume visits with Chad and stay overnight at their house. Emily did not give up on this issue or pretend in any way. They were already putting Hope through too much with the rouse and would not put any more on her. She knew it angered Chad and Veronica that Hope still called Shawn dad. Shawn had limited time with Hope, only occasionally taking her after school.

Emily explained to Veronica that each time the subject was brought up that Shawn was the only dad Hope knew. And if she forced her to stop talking to him and accept Chad, that would only worsen things. They just had to be patient and let Hope make her own decision. Veronica never cared much for this answer, but never pushed it further.

With fall already upon them and winter around the corner, she had plenty to do to prepare. With so much work, it only made it harder to have an assistant, so she gave fake work to do and then redid it at night herself. She wanted Veronica to believe she was putting

more and more trust in her, but didn't really trust
her with anything going on in Sanctuary.
The reports always matched what she did
herself for the first month.

However, shortly after, things began to
change. The inventory reports started showing
fewer and fewer items, the work reports showed
less being done, and the only people who
showed to be pulling close to their fair share of
work were Veronica and Chad. She knew that
this was wrong, but let Veronica think she
believed it. She could only see two reasons to
falsify the information. First, it painted Chad
and Veronica in the best light. Second, it would
force them to do another run outside the wall.

They had not done this in some time. The
plan was to make Sanctuary self-sufficient so
that runs were no longer needed. However,
Veronica's version of the report showed that
they would run out of essentials if they didn't do
it soon. Emily pretended to be worried about
each passing day. Today was no different as she
reviewed the completed false reports. She
flipped through the pages, acting concerned and
frustrated with each.

"What the hell are they doing?!" Emily
exclaimed, dropping the reports on the desk.

"They want you to fail," Veronica replied
quickly. "If you fail, they can put someone else
in charge."

"They couldn't if they wanted to!" Emily
said with all the anger she could muster.

"It's evident that they believe otherwise," Veronica said, motioning to the reports.

A knock on the door stopped her from responding, and she was thankful. She hated these conversations where she had to play the part of the angry dictator.

"Come in!" Emily called out, turning to the door.

"I'm sorry to bother you," Jacob said as he walked in. "I must follow up on my request for additional hands on the farm."

"Additional hands?" Emily replied, genuinely confused.

"I had spoken with Ms. Veronica last week," Jacob replied, ashamed. "Our crops produced more than we could have predicted. We need help getting them harvested, gathered, and stored. If we wait much longer, they will spoil in the fields."

She immediately looked at Veronica. She had been so careful to keep track of things herself, but this was one thing she could not control.

"You have already been assigned more than enough people," Veronica replied. "It's your job to assign them more hours and get the work done."

"We have all been working to exhaustion," Jacob replied with a twinge of anger in his voice.

"Then it should be done," Veronica shot back.

"But if it doesn't get done, everyone hurts," Emily replied calmly.

"I wouldn't be here if we weren't out of time," Jacob said, trying to calm himself down. "If we don't finish it today, we will lose our window."

"Then I suggest you figure it out!" Veronica yelled, slamming her hand on the desk. "Or we will find someone who will!"

"You know what?!" Jacob yelled back.

"Jacob!" Emily yelled, stopping the fight. "Wait for me outside."

Jacob looked back at Veronica with nothing but hatred before turning and leaving.

"You're going to let him get away with that!" Veronica yelled as soon as the door shut. "Do you know how to run a farm?" Emily asked, looking at Veronica.

"Of course not," Veronica sneered back.

"Neither do I," Emily admitted. "We're lucky that the animals survived at all. Jacob is the only person inside these walls who knows how to do it. It's not like we have many options."

"So, he gets to be lazy," Veronica said with cold eyes.

"We can either get him the help he needs or starve," Emily replied. "I'm not going to let my child starve for any reason."

"Neither will I," Veronica sighed.

"These are things you need to learn," Emily calmly said. "We are going to need to do a run soon, and I hoped to leave you in charge while I was gone."

"Really?!" Veronica said with excitement.

"I needed someone for more than filling out reports," Emily sighed. "But maybe I should...."

"I can do better," Veronica quickly said. "You can trust me with the code."

"The code is out of the question," Emily replied. "I've never shared that and have no intentions of ever doing so."

This wasn't a lie. While Hope did know the code, she had never shared it with her.

"I just need someone to run things while I'm gone," Emily continued.

"I can do that," Veronica smiled. "And I'm sure one day you'll see that I can be trusted with the code."

"Maybe," Emily lied, trying to ignore the sick feeling in her stomach.

"Do you want me to call in some extra hands to help the farm?" Veronica asked.

"Let me see how bad it is first," Emily replied, walking towards the door. "Then we will come up with a plan."

She walked out of the office, closing the door behind her. Marley stood up from where he was lying by the council table. He refused to be in the office with Veronica and waited here for her each day. She patted his head as he walked over to join her. She found Jacob waiting outside, still fuming from his argument with Veronica.

"I don't know what else she wants us to do!" Jacob yelled as soon as she walked out. "My kids have been falling asleep in the fields. They are working so hard!"

"I'm sorry," Emily gently replied. "I didn't know."

"If you want an assistant, I'm good with that!" Jacob continued to yell. "You work too hard, and I think you need help! But her?!"

"I can't explain it," Emily replied, looking down at her shoes. "I can only help fix this now."

"I don't know if you can," Jacob sighed. "It would take almost everyone to finish the job tonight."

"Then I will shut down everything nonessential and get you, everyone," Emily replied.

"Not her," Jacob growled, glaring back into the town hall.

"Agreed," Emily nodded. "And from now on, come to me with everything."

"You weren't there, and I didn't want to bother you at home," Jacob said, calming down.

"Please," Emily said, looking at him. "Please bother me at home."

"Right," Jacob nodded.

She could tell he was still frustrated, but was done yelling.

"You head back, and I'll be there with help as quick as I can," Emily said. "We will get this fixed."

"Yeah," Jacob half-laughed as he walked away.

She headed inside and quickly told Veronica what the plan was. Veronica looked relieved when she said she had the rest of the day off, but Chad would be required to help with extra credits. She and Marley then quickly made their way to the COM building.

"I need to get with all the leads and enact a state of emergency," Emily said to Sarah as she walked in.

"What kind of emergency?" Sarah asked with concern.

"The kind where we get everyone we can to the farm before losing our crop," Emily sighed.

"Right," Sarah nodded without hesitation. Emily watched as she looked at Margaret.

"Everyone, please report to the main street except for those on the wall," Margaret said, the announcement echoing through the speakers.

"Thank you," Emily said as she turned back outside with Marley.

It only took a few moments for everyone to gather, each looking confused. Jacob made his way next to her, ready to help her organize the effort. Though it was technically fall, the sun was still beating down on them.

"There are crops in the field that need to be harvested, gathered, and stored by the end of today," Emily said as loudly as she could to the crowd. "Jacobs' crew has tried their best to get it done, but needs our help. If we don't get it done, we will all go without.

"How much time do we have?" Someone in the crowd yelled out.

"This afternoon," Emily sighed. "The short time is my fault. I didn't know the situation."

"There's nothing that can be done about that now," Jacob spoke up as some grumbled through the crowd. "We are family, and family supports each other."

"We will all make our way to the farm and get this done," Emily spoke, smiling at Jacob. "We will keep to the wall schedule. So, please report on time unless Shawn tells you you are not needed. Jacob's crew will tell each of you where you are needed."

She watched as no one questioned her, and the crowd started to make their way to the farm. She turned to join them when she was suddenly stopped.

"I can't do much walking or lifting," Margaret replied. "But I can drive a truck."

"Are you sure?" Emily asked with concern.

"I'm tougher than I look," Margaret smiled back at her.

"Oh, I know," Emily laughed. "We'd better get going."

She and Margaret made their way to the farm. Jacob was already dividing everyone up and putting them to work.

"Margaret will need to drive a truck," Emily said as she walked toward him.

"No problem," Jacob smiled. "Are you up to loading?"

"You're the boss," Emily nodded... "You tell me what to do."

"The west field is harvested, and the crates are sitting in rows. I've sent some people there. If Margaret drives, they can hand you the crates to stack," Jacob explained.

"We're on it," Emily nodded.

She and Margaret walked over to the flatbed truck. She climbed onto the back while Margaret took her place in the driver's seat. It didn't take them long to arrive at the field. Margaret slowed the truck to a crawl. She began taking the crates from people and stacking them in the truck. When the bed was full, Margaret drove them back to the farm. She would hand off the crates to be stored, and then they returned to the field.

The hours passed quickly under the hot sun. Her body was begging for a break, but she refused. She had put Veronica in a position to cause this mess and would do whatever she had to do to fix it. The truck bed was only half full when she felt it stop.

"Is something wrong?" Emily called up Margaret.

"You need a drink," Hope's voice came from beside the truck.

"I've got a lot of work to do," Emily smiled back at her with sweat pouring down her face.

"And if you don't take a drink, you'll pass out, and then it won't get done," Hope said firmly, holding a cup of water.

"Yes, ma'am," Emily said as she sat on the truck bed.

Hope handed her the cup of water and then moved on. She drank the water slowly and watched. Hope and the other children were making their way through the field, ensuring each person stopped and took a drink. She couldn't help but smile. The adults were making this place what it was, but not for themselves. It was for the children. The children who were now out under the harsh sun found their own way to contribute to the needed work.

She continued to smile as she finished her water. She then returned the empty cup to Margaret and was ready to return to work. The truck started slowly moving forward again, and she began to stack the crates. The work continued with a few mandatory water breaks. She felt like she would fall over as she handed her last crate off, and the work was finally done. She slid down to sit on the bed and allowed her legs to dangle over the edge. Margaret climbed out of the cab and walked towards her.

"You okay, dear?" Margaret asked, looking at her with concern.

"Never better," Emily replied, exhausted.

"Things haven't been right here since, well, you know," Margaret said, looking off into the distance.

Emily followed her gaze and saw Shawn. His shirt was off, and, from the looks of it, he had been working in the fields all day. She had been so busy that she hadn't even noticed that he was here.

"I know," Emily replied, forcing herself to look away from him. "It's just how things have to be."

"But not how you want them to be," Margaret smiled at her.

"I…" Emily started to reply, realizing what she had done.

"Don't," Margaret interrupted her. "You always do what's best. Just know, we all trust you."

She didn't know what to say. She couldn't tell Margaret the truth, but couldn't lie to her.

"You'd better get home and get some rest," Margaret smiled. "You've got a lot of work to do tomorrow."

She nodded and watched as Margaret walked away. She couldn't believe what had just happened. She had been so careful not to have a word slip like that. No one could know what she and Shawn were doing if their plan was going to work. The exhaustion was the only excuse she had. While she had not told Margaret everything, she had given away just enough. It also told her that there were people in Sanctuary who knew she was up to something.

She was too tired to deal with these thoughts right now. Instead, she forced herself to slide off the truck, her legs weak under her as she stood. She would be walking home alone tonight. Marley would be at home with Hope, waiting for her to arrive. She began to walk slowly away towards home.

"We got it done," Jacob said as he came running towards her.

"We saved it all?" Emily asked him.

"Every last thing," Jacob smiled.

"That's amazing," Emily replied, feeling joy for the first time in months.

"I wanted to apologize for losing my temper earlier," Jacob said, looking more serious. "I know you are stressed right now, and I didn't mean to add to it."

"I just want you to know you can always come to me," Emily replied. "No matter what it is."

"I do," Jacob nodded. "Now, I think we both need to get some sleep."

"Definitely," Emily laughed. "I'll see you tomorrow."

Jacob simply nodded and began towards the farmhouse. She made her way slowly home, each step feeling more and more painful.

"Emily!" Chad's voice called out as she was reaching for the handle.

"Is everything alright?" Emily asked, turning back towards him.

"I have to talk to you," Chad said, running towards her and joining her on the porch.

She stood frozen as he approached her and took her hand.

"Watching you today just reminded me why I love you," Chad said softly.

"Go home, Chad," Emily said, trying to pull her hand back.

"Veronica and I are separating," Chad smiled. "We agree that we aren't supposed to be together."

"If you're serious," Emily began. "I'll assign you to an apartment."

"Alright," Chad replied, still smiling. "And I'm sure you'll ask Veronica about it tomorrow."

"It's really none of my business," Emily replied. "Let me just check which apartments are open."

She felt Chad pull her towards him and stood in shock for less than a moment as he kissed her. She pushed him back and opened and stepped inside her door.

"Just pick one, and I'll mark it as taken tomorrow," Emily said as quickly as possible.

"I could stay," Chad said as he stepped forward.

"Hope's home," Emily said quickly. "Good night."

She closed the door and turned to the living room.

"What was that?" Shawn asked.

She nearly jumped out of her skin.

"What are you doing here?" Emily smiled at him.

"I came to tell you that I couldn't do this anymore," Shawn said sternly. "Hope is at your mom's for the night."

"You know he does this every few months," Emily said, not understanding why Shawn seemed mad at her.

"Veronica stopped me on my way here, telling me how she and I had something in common," Shawn said flatly. "That we both had to let go of someone to let them be with who they were supposed to."

"I will let the dead eat me alive before I accept that I'm supposed to be with him!" Emily heard herself yell. "The only reason I didn't deck him for doing that was part of our stupid plan."

Shawn, acting jealous every time Chad lost his mind and tried to get her to be with him again, was more than she could take. She knew she only loved one person, and that was Shawn.

"You must stop reacting like this every time," Emily continued. "I have been dying a little every day without you."

"I thought I could let it go," Shawn said, clenching his teeth. "But I can't."

"What do you want me to do?" Emily heard herself pleading with him.

"I can't tell you what to do," Shawn replied, softening just a little. "I can only tell you what I can't do."

She looked at him and couldn't help but fear what he was getting ready to say.

"I can't do this anymore," Shawn continued. "I can't be with you and watch him try to get you back every chance he gets, and I can't pretend that we aren't together while finding a small way to say I love you."

"What are you saying?" Emily said with tears in her eyes.

"I'm saying it's over," Shawn replied shortly.

"Shawn," Emily said as she took a step forward.

She stopped as Shawn took a step back. She looked at him and saw no sign of love and affection in his eyes. They were cold and serious.

"This isn't another act," Shawn said as he stepped around her and opened the door.

She couldn't say anything as she watched him walk out and close the door. She was in such a state of shock that she couldn't even cry.

Instead, she just stood, staring at the door and praying he would walk back through it.

Chapter 7

Emily made her way through the next few months on autopilot. She did her day-to-day work, but it was more out of habit than drive. She had tried several times to talk to Shawn, but he pushed her away each time. She couldn't understand what had happened. Was it his jealousy or insecurities about Chad that really ended their relationship?

"Where did you go?" Joe asked, pulling her back to her conversation.

"Sorry," Emily replied. "I just have a lot on my mind."

"Mom just wanted me to remind you that we will all be at your place tomorrow," Joe said with a slight smile.

"Tomorrow?" Emily asked, confused.

She wasn't sure what month it was, let alone what significance tomorrow had.

"Thanksgiving," Joe replied with concern. "Are you sure you're alright?"

"Yeah," Emily smiled, trying to play it off. "My mind is just all over the place."

"Maybe you should talk about it?" Joe offered with concern.

"Maybe later," Emily smiled. "I'd better go get the rest of the stuff for tomorrow."

"Do you remember what you're getting?"
Joe teased.

"Yes," Emily laughed, rolling her eyes.
"I'll see you tomorrow."

"If you don't forget!" Joe called after her.

She quickly made her way to the store
with Marley. Hope was off playing with the
other Sanctuary kids while the parents prepared
for the next day. She opened the door to the
store as Marley took his post outside.

"I thought you may have forgotten,"
Jessica teased as she began to set her bags on
the counter.

"I almost did," Emily laughed as she
handed over her credit card.

She waited while Jessica ran the card and
handed it back to her.

"Where's your assistant?" Jessica asked,
looking around.

"Gave her the day off," Emily replied
with a sigh of relief. "I just needed a day to
gather myself."

"I don't blame you," Jessica nodded. She
could tell there was something Jessica wanted to
ask, but she was holding back.

"Alright," Emily smiled, sliding her card
into her pocket. "What's going on?"

"I was just wondering if you ever found
out more about that list?" Jessica said in almost
a whisper. "I expected there to be a council
meeting over it. But then you and Shawn ended
things, and well…."

She had nearly forgotten that Jessica was the only person outside her and Shawn who knew about the list. She had been so caught up in the fake breakup turned real, and her detective work, she never did give Jessica any explanation.

"I'm trying to get her to let something slip," Emily admitted. "She's getting more comfortable, so hopefully, we should know something soon."

"I still think we should have a meeting," Jessica replied.

"Just so everyone knows to keep an eye out."

"We will do it after the holiday," Emily smiled.

"I know it will suck because you have to sit there with Shawn, but I think we need this," Jessica continued, almost as if she had not heard her.

"Jessica," Emily laughed. "I agree with you. I'll set one up after the holiday."

"Oh," Jessica smiled. "I had a whole speech planned."

"I'm sure it was amazing, but you already sold me," Emily laughed. "I'll talk to you on Friday."

"See you on Friday," Jessica smiled as she grabbed her bags and walked outside.

The wind was cooler, but they were nowhere near the harshest part of winter. She and Marley made their way home, where she quickly put away the groceries. She then spent the next few hours prepping what they could for the next day. She had just finished when Hope came bursting through the door.

"Mommy!" Hope yelled.

"Hope!" Emily replied as she ran to the living room. She could hear the panic in Hope's voice. "What's wrong?"

"You can't make me!" Hope yelled at her as soon as she saw her. She could see that it wasn't panic now, but anger.

"I can't make you what?" Emily asked, confused.

"You can't make me call him dad!" Hope yelled. "You can't make me stop calling Shawn dad, and you can't make me live with him!"

"What are you talking about?" Emily replied, searching for an explanation for Hope's accusations.

"I saw him on my way home, and he told me everything!" Hope yelled with tears running down her face.

"Who did you see, and what did he tell you?" Emily asked.

She felt that Chad was trying again to force himself into their lives.

"I saw daddy!" Hope yelled. "I asked him if he was coming to dinner tomorrow."

She felt confusion and anger wash over her as Hope spoke. She realized that it hadn't been Chad that had upset Hope, but Shawn.

"He told me how you and Chad have been dating," Hope continued to cry. "And you guys were just trying to find the right time to tell me so he could move into our home."

"Hope," Emily started.

"He also told me that I need to stay away from him and stop calling him dad," Hope continued.

"Anything else?" Emily asked, trying to control her temper.

"Isn't that enough?!" Hope cried.

"More than," Emily nodded. "I don't know why he said those things to you. I am not dating Chad, and he will not be moving into this house."

"Then why doesn't Shawn want me to be his daughter anymore?" Hope cried.

"Stay with Marley," Emily said as she walked past Hope and out the front door.

She could see blurs of people around her as she walked and the muffled voices. However, none of them belonged to her current target, so they never came into focus. She made her way up the wall and, after walking around, still did not find her target.

"Emily!" Sam called after her, grabbing her by the shoulder before she could head down the stairs.

"Where is he?" Emily growled at him.

"Who?" Sam asked, taking a step back from her.

"Shawn," Emily asked, just as hateful.

"Emily," Sam said, obviously trying to calm her down. "I don't know what's going on, but...."

"He hurt Hope," Emily interrupted. "Where is he?"

"He said he was going home," Sam said with a look of shock. "Is Hope okay?"

"She's in tears," Emily snarled as she headed down the stairs, barely feeling the steps under her feet.

She made her way to the apartments and didn't stop to knock on Shawn's door. She turned the knob and threw the door open harder than she intended.

"That didn't take long," Shawn said without looking at her from where he was sitting on the couch.

"What the hell is wrong with you!?" Emily launched at him.

"It's not the first time we have had to hurt her to protect her," Shawn replied coldly as he took a drink. He looked to be holding a jar of moonshine.

"How the fuck are you protecting her?!" Emily continued to yell.

Shawn said nothing and took another drink.

"You want to hurt me, fine!" Emily continued. "But she is innocent! You promised her you would always protect her!"

"That's what I'm doing!" Shawn said, slamming the jar down on the table.

"How?!" Emily asked.

"It's safer for her to hate me and stay away," Shawn said, rubbing his face. "It's safer for both of you."

She still felt her anger boiling inside her, but couldn't help but be confused.

"I'm tired of this game," Emily sighed. "We are always lying and hurting each other to protect someone."

"That's what you think?!" Shawn said, looking at her for the first time. "That this is a fucking game!"

She paused as she looked at his face. Shawn was not one to cry, but she could tell he had been crying before she arrived.

"What is going on?" Emily pleaded with him.

"Just get out!" Shawn yelled, looking back down at his boots. "And don't come back."

She turned and slammed the door behind her as she left. She felt the energy and the anger that had given her drain from her body as she walked back out of the apartments. She didn't understand everything that was going on, but there was one thing she knew for sure now. Shawn was in trouble.

"Emily!" Alec yelled as he walked up beside her. "Sam said you were looking for Shawn, that he had hurt Hope."

"I found him," Emily replied as she continued to walk.

"What's going on?" Alec asked, stepping in front of her.

"This is what he wanted," Emily said to herself.

"What?" Alec asked, looking confused.

"He pushed us both away and knew I would let it slip that he hurt Hope. That would turn everyone against him and keep everyone away," Emily continued to herself.

"Emily," Alec said firmly. "What's going on?"

"Shawn's in trouble," Emily finally replied, looking at him.

"What kind of trouble?" Alec asked, concerned.

"The kind where he thinks it's not safe for anyone to be near him," Emily explained. "That it's safer for everyone to hate him than to stand beside him."

"I have no idea what that means," Alec said.

"Can you gather the rest of the council and ask them to come to my house?" Emily asked, her mind racing to form a plan. "Not Shawn, and don't use the walkies," she quickly added.

"What should I tell them?" Alec asked, looking confused.

"Just say I want to check in with everyone before the holiday," Emily replied. "I promise, I'll explain everything once everyone is there."

"I'm on it," Alec smiled as he headed into town.

She took off at a run towards her family's houses. She was breathing hard as she finally caught sight of Rachael.

"Rachael!" Emily called out.

"Emily?" Rachael said with concern as she turned to face her. "What's going on?"

"I need you to get the rest of the family and meet me at my place," Emily said through panting breaths.

"Is someone hurt?" Rachael asked, grabbing her shoulder.

"I need your help," Emily breathed. "But first, I have to tell you all the truth."

Rachael said nothing and instead took off towards their parents' house. Emily turned and ran back home. Hope was sitting on the couch with Marley's head in her lap. Tears were still running down her face, but she was much calmer than when she had left.

"I'm going to fix this," Emily assured her. "Can you help me move some extra chairs into the dining room?"

"Why?" Hope asked, wiping her face.

"I've called in some help," Emily said as she walked towards the dining room.

She heard Hope and Marley climb off the couch. They moved the extra chairs from the kitchen and office into the dining room.

"Mommy, what's going on?" Hope asked when they had finished.

The front door opened, and she could hear that everyone had arrived.

"I'll explain in just a minute," Emily assured her.

Hope guided everyone into the dining room while she gathered a few things from her office. They were silent and seated when she returned, waiting for her.

"I want to start with I'm sorry," Emily began.

"For what?" Julia asked without hesitation. "I'm not good with all this cloak and dagger stuff."

"A few months ago, Jessica discovered a list in the store's back room during the storm," Emily began. "It looked like Veronica was gathering large amounts of supplies, more than she could ever use. We needed to find out why, so I made her my assistant, hoping she would let something slip."

"That makes more sense now," Cole nodded.

"When we weren't getting anywhere," Emily continued. "Shawn and I devised a plan. We would make them think that their plan to get Shawn and me out of the picture was working. The breakup was fake."

"We all thought something was up," Doc spoke. "You guys have fought before, but it seemed out of character."

"If it was fake, why isn't Daddy here?" Hope asked. "Why did he say those things to me?"

"The night after the crop harvest," Emily continued. "I came home to find Shawn here after Chad tried to get me to take him back and kissed me on the porch. I sent him packing and went inside."

"He did what?!" Charlie asked angrily.

"That's not what's important," Emily said, waving her hands. "When I got inside, Shawn said that he had come to call off the fake breakup. But after seeing what Chad had done, he decided to make it real and permanent."

"I talked to him that day," Joe spoke up. "He was talking about needing to set things straight. It didn't make any sense. I just thought he was talking about getting you guys back together."

"Today, he did something to ensure he pushed everyone away," Emily continued. "He pushed Hope away and made sure to do it in a way that would upset her."

"Just to play devil's advocate," Alec spoke up. "How do we know he's in trouble? Maybe he's just decided this is how he wants things."

"When I went to see him, he had been crying," Emily explained. "If he truly wanted this, it wouldn't hurt him enough to make him fall apart."

"What did he say while you were there?" Christine asked.

"He was drinking, and his eyes were red from tears," Emily described. "He said it was safer for everyone to stay away from him. It made him really angry when I told him I was done playing this game with him. Other than that, he just looked broken."

"What would Shawn be so scared of here?" Sam asked.

"We've all seen him come toe to toe with nasty stuff, but nothing has made him give up like this."

"Especially while trying to make things safe around here," Sarah added.

"I don't know," Emily sighed. "It could be part of what Veronica is planning or something else entirely."

"We can't help him if we don't know what it is," Rachael said.

"Maybe he can't talk inside the walls," Joe offered. "We could do a run and take only those we know he can trust."

"We are actually fine on supplies," Emily said, dismissing the idea. "The reports that Veronica has been doing are all falsified to make it worse than it really is. I have been redoing them on my own."

"That's all the more reason to do it," Jessica said. "We can accomplish two things at once. Help Shawn and prove to Veronica that you are trusting her."

"It's a big risk for anyone who goes,"
Emily replied. "I can't ask anyone to take it."

"You never do," Julia smiled. "But we're
doing it anyway."

"We'll call an official meeting after the
holidays. You bring the list of supplies Veronica
says are low on and plan it," Alec spoke. "Make
sure she is there, and I'll ensure Shawn is."

"I understand, Shawn, but why her?"
Emily asked.

"It will show her how much faith you put
in her, especially when we all object to saying
the supplies aren't low," Alec explained. "And
we can see how tense things are between him
and her."

"Mommy," Hope spoke suddenly. "We
have to save Daddy."

"Of course," Emily smiled at her.

"We're family," Julia smiled. "And none
of us will let someone tear our family apart."
"Couldn't have said it better myself," Charlie
smiled.

"We'd better all get going," Sarah spoke.
"The council first and family after. We don't
want this to look suspicious."

"Be sure to grumble as you leave about
me," Emily smiled. "Just to play off that you
guys aren't happy about what I had to say."

"We can play it up," Cole offered. "You
evil dictator."

Everyone shared a laugh as they walked
to the door. Once the door was open, all of their

moods changed. She could have sworn that they all hated her if she didn't know better. She and her family remained silent until the door closed.

"Just a thought," Charlie spoke first. "Maybe remove Shawn from the head of security until this is figured out."

"You think someone might try to use that position against him?" Emily asked.

"It's all he really has left," Charlie offered. "You could appoint Alec temporarily."

"Veronica has been pushing me to remove him," Emily added. "I will have to think on this and see how things go."

"Understandable," Christine nodded.

"I don't want to have Thanksgiving or Christmas without Daddy," Hope said firmly. "He's always here."

"We have to," Emily comforted her. "We have to act like everything is normal to protect daddy."

"Why do adults always do things that hurt people to protect them?" Hope asked, frustrated. "It doesn't make sense."

"I hear you, kid," Joe laughed. "But your mom is pretty smart. I think we should trust her on this."

"We'll have another Thanksgiving and Christmas after all of this is fixed," Christine offered. "To celebrate the family being back together."

"First, we save Daddy," Hope said. "Then we celebrate."

Chapter 8

Everyone tried their best to be cheerful for the next month, but behind the large wooden door of her house, the worry hung thick in the air. Emily lay in bed at night with Hope and Marley, unable to sleep. Both tossed and turned as if the worry was haunting their dreams. She did her best to comfort them, but in the end, nothing worked.

February finally came, and it was time to implement their plan. The plan was in place, and she couldn't sleep the night before. She and Hope went through their morning routine without a word. Hope was dressed and ready to go to Christine and Charlie's for the day.

"It's time to make the call," Hope reminded her, her tiny voice shattering the silence.

"You're right," Emily sighed as she grabbed her walkie. "The council will be meeting at ten today at town hall. All members are required to attend."

"You think he'll come?" Hope asked Emily as she returned the walkie to her waist. "I hope so," Emily smiled.

She took Hope by the hand and walked

out the door with her and Marley. Hope didn't feel that she could be at this council meeting. Hope understood without asking that it would be safer if she didn't come.

She dropped Hope off with Christine and Charlie without a word. Everyone knew what was happening and didn't want to say something that shouldn't be heard. She made her way to the town hall.

"Good morning," Veronica smiled at her as she entered.

"If you say so," Emily replied as she made her way to the office while Marley took his spot under the council table.

"Bad night?" Veronica asked.

"I looked over the reports most of the time," Emily lied. "We have to do a run."

"Would you like me to announce a meeting?" Veronica smiled.

"I already did," Emily answered. "Everyone should be here at ten." "What would you like me to do?" Veronica asked with way too much enthusiasm.

"You're going to join us," Emily answered. "I want you to sit beside me."

"Isn't that where the head of security is supposed to sit?" Veronica asked.

Emily could hear the excitement in her voice.

"Normally," Emily answered. "But I need someone in that seat I can trust."

"You are finally letting him go," Veronica nearly squealed with excitement.

"Maybe," Emily replied.

"You know who I think would be a good choice?" Veronica continued.

"Alec," Emily interrupted her.

"I think that would be worse than Shawn," Veronica said with a look on her face like she had just drunk spoiled milk.

"He knows the job, the transition would be smooth, and I trust him," Emily sighed.

"But his wife is crazy," Veronica blurted out.

"Aren't we all?" Emily laughed, genuinely finding humor in her own words.

She and Veronica worked for the next few hours, making a list of supplies they would need to gather on the run. Once they were finished, they went out to the council table and sat to wait for everyone. Marley moved from his position under the table to by the door. "I think that dog is getting too old," Veronica remarked as Marley moved.

"He's fine," Emily said without a glance.

They didn't have to wait long for everyone to arrive. Everyone made the appropriate glares and whispers about where Veronica was sitting. When Shawn arrived, he simply leaned against the wall, seemingly unfazed by the situation.

"We have a problem," Emily said to them all. "At first, I thought maybe the numbers were wrong, but I redid them all myself yesterday. Our supplies in every department are too low to get us through winter."

"That's impossible!" Jacob blurted out. "We have more food than ever before!"

"You reported our lowest crop yet," Emily replied. "So, unless you held some back for yourself...."

"How dare you!" Jacob spat back.

She knew this was what they planned, but it still hurt her to talk to him like this.

"Our construction supply is more than ample," Jose spoke next. "I have to agree with Jacob that the numbers are wrong."

"I'm not going to argue this!" Emily yelled as everyone began to talk at once. "We have to do a run if we are going to survive."

"When?" Shawn asked, not looking at anyone.

"Today," Emily replied. "I'll give you a few hours to get ready, and we'll head out."

"There's no way we will make it back before dark," Sam said with concern.

"Then get ready faster," Emily replied shortly. "I expect the normal team to be ready."

Everyone stood angrily from the table and turned to leave.

"Shawn, Alec, I need you both to stay a moment," Emily said, bracing herself.

Shawn leaned back against the wall while Alec took his seat once more. Everyone else filed out, and Veronica remained where she was. She waited until everyone was gone to speak.

"The only way for us to be this low on supplies is if people are stealing them," Emily said, looking at Shawn. "It's your job to keep an eye on these things."

"You know about the only attempted theft," Shawn glared at her.

"Convenient," Emily huffed. "Until I can figure out what's going on, Alec will be taking over as head of security."

"What?" Alec said, surprised.

She had not had time to warn him about this decision beforehand. She hoped he would understand.

"I'm still going on the run," Shawn said coldly.

"Fine," Emily nodded. "Give Alec all the information and your keys. You will report to him moving forward."

Shawn didn't hesitate and laid all his keys on the table.

"I'll meet you at the security office to give you the rundown," Shawn said to Alec.

"I don't want this," Alec said to Shawn and then looked back at Emily.

"It's actually the smartest thing she's ever done," Shawn replied before walking out.

"Did he just admit to helping people steal?" Veronica asked, surprised.

"I don't know," Emily sighed. "I don't have time for this. Alec, you should get to work."

Alec stood without a word and headed out of the building.

"While I'm gone, I need you to…." Emily began.

"Watch Hope?" Veronica asked hopefully.

"Make sure everyone stays on task," Emily said, shaking her head. "Alec will be with me, so I need someone I can trust to ensure that nothing else goes missing."

"I can do that," Veronica smiled.

"Hope will stay with my parents," Emily continued. "She's had a rough few days, but when I get back, we'll see about her spending more time with you, Chad, and her brother."

"I would like them to get to know each other," Veronica smiled. "They are still siblings even if neither of us is with their father anymore."

"My thoughts exactly," Emily nodded. "I should get my gear together."

"Don't worry about a thing," Veronica assured her. "I can handle this while you're gone."

She said nothing else as she stood and left. Marley followed her out, and they made the walk home together. She grabbed her backpack that Hope had helped her prepare that morning. Everything was already packed and ready. She looked down at Marley as she slung the bag onto her back.

"You're not getting too old, are you, boy?" Emily smiled at him.

Marley began wagging his tail excitedly.

"But maybe you should stay here," Emily said as she knelt to pet him. "I've got plenty of people watching my back out there."

Marley cocked his head to the side as if he were confused.

"If the threat is in here, I need you to keep everyone safe," Emily continued. "Can you keep them safe?"

Marley barked excitedly and began to bounce around.

"Good boy," Emily smiled as she stood up. "We'd better get going."

She headed out the door with Marley, shutting it behind them.

"Go to Hope," Emily instructed Marley.

Marley took off instantly at a run towards Charlie and Christine's house. She didn't follow but walked slowly towards the gate. Everyone was busy, and Alec was trying his best to organize everyone. Apparently, they were all in agreement to leave early. She looked around and was surprised to see Joe and Rachael among the crowd.

"What are you two doing?" Emily asked as she walked toward them.

"We volunteered," Rachael said as she turned towards Emily.

"It's not safe out there," Emily said with concern.

"You don't have to tell us that," Joe laughed. "We were out there a lot longer than you."

"What he's trying to say," Rachael said, rolling her eyes. "Is that we can handle ourselves. Alec said we would have to stick with him, so I'm sure we'll be fine."

"I don't know," Emily said, looking around.

"You're not asking," Joe winked at her. "And neither are we."

She knew what he was referencing and that she had no chance of winning this fight.

"Just stay with Alec," She finally replied. "Mom will kill me if anything happens to you two."

"You got it, boss," Joe said as they saluted her.

"Shit," Emily heard herself laugh.

She knew that the two of them going was risky, but part of her was glad to have them there nonetheless. She made her way over to her SUV, where Cole was already sitting behind the wheel.

"Thought I would drive," Cole smiled as she opened the door.

"Good call," Emily smiled. "I'm likely to fall asleep."

"Figured as much," Cole nodded. "You can curl up in the back with Marley if you want."

"He's staying here," Emily said as she tossed her bag in.

"Well, it will be just you and me then," Cole smiled.

"You not mad at me like the others?" Emily asked, realizing that their conversation could be heard by too many people.

"Nah," Cole smiled. "Life's too short for all that, especially these days. I reckon it's best just to get the job done and move on."

"I wish everyone thought that way," Emily said, looking around.

No one questioned her anymore, but the looks said things louder than words ever could.

"They'll get there," Cole smiled.

"I hope so," Emily smiled back as she tossed her bag into the backseat.

She shut the SUV door and began walking to the control panel. Everyone looked to be about ready to go. She scanned the crowd as she walked and noticed that Shawn was missing.

"Alec!" Emily hollered to get his attention. "Is everyone ready?"

"Just waiting on Shawn," Alec replied.

"Who's he riding with?" Emily asked as innocently as she could.

She knew that Shawn wasn't riding with her, but wanted to ensure it was with someone he trusted.

"No one," Alec yelled back. "He said he's driving himself."

Alec then nodded towards the gate where Shawn was pushing the motorcycle through. She suddenly understood what he meant. The point of this was to give Shawn a chance to talk. That wasn't going to happen with him on that thing.

"That's a bit loud to be driving out there," Emily said as she walked toward him.

"Good if we get in a pinch," Shawn said as he kept walking. "I can draw them away."

"Doesn't sound good for you," Emily replied, trying to hide the concern in her voice.

"Alec already approved it," Shawn said hatefully. "Besides, what happens to me is really none of your business."

"You're right," Emily shot back out of anger. "Do whatever the hell you want."

"That's the plan," Shawn said as he climbed on the motorcycle.

"Stubborn ass," Emily said as she walked to the control panel and entered the code.

She heard the bike roar to life over the other vehicle's engines as the gate began to move. She followed the line of cars out on foot, closing the gate behind them. Once the gate was closed, she climbed into the SUV with Cole.

"This isn't the plan," Cole said as he put the SUV in the drive.

"None of my plans ever work," Emily sighed.

"We'll figure it out," Cole assured her.

"Yeah, and that new plan will probably blow up in my face, too," Emily sighed.

"Hey, you might not get all the details right on the first try, but you always manage to get the job done," Cole smiled at her.

"It's easy with you guys around," Emily smiled back.

"I'll pair myself with him for the search parties," Cole said, turning the SUV onto the blacktop road. "I'll get him to talk if I gotta beat it out of him."

She couldn't help but laugh at the mental image she got. While Cole was strong enough, Shawn was way bigger them him. It would be a David and Goliath fight.

"Hopefully, it won't come to that," Emily laughed.

"Just saying, if it does, I've got this," Cole smiled. "Us country folk are tougher than we look."

"I know it," Emily smiled.

She turned her attention to the outside of the SUV window. It had been a while since she had been this far away from Sanctuary. That trip had not gone to plan either. But they had managed to save a group of girls. Maybe Cole was right. Even if things weren't going how she wanted, it didn't mean that nothing good couldn't come out of this trip.

She let her mind rest while the trees blurred by, not focusing on any of them. Suddenly, she caught a glimpse of a pair of eyes staring back at her. She forced herself to focus on them. They were definitely living, with no milky white coating. The way they looked back at her, though, made her uncomfortable. She felt herself jump, and a gasp escaped her mouth.

"What's wrong?" Cole asked, concerned.

"There's someone there," Emily replied. "Stop the truck."

Cole didn't hesitate and hit the brakes. She reached to open the door as soon as the SUV stopped.

"Wait!" Cole yelled as he grabbed her arm. "You can't just go running out there like everything is normal."

"If they need help or maybe saw the signs," Emily explained, looking back at him.

"Or if the danger is outside the walls instead of in," Cole added. "That could be a scout instead of a person in need."

"Everything alright up there?" Alec's voice came over the radio.

"Emily saw someone in the woods on the right-hand side," Cole responded. "She wants us to check it out."

"On it," Alec answered.

"It's a waste of time," Shawn's voice suddenly rang out. She could hear the worry in his words. "She probably just saw one of the dead. We should keep moving and not waste time."

She looked at Cole and could see that he was thinking the same thing she was. Since when did Shawn not investigate something like this? Something wasn't right, and it could be the thing that had Shawn so scared.

"Check it out anyway," Emily replied into the walkie.

The walkie remained silent as everyone climbed out, weapons in hand, and began to search the wood line. They searched for about fifteen minutes before anyone spoke.

"Just a zombie," Shawn said with concern and frustration.

"I saw the eyes," Emily insisted. "They were alive."

"Maybe you're just seeing things," Shawn huffed as he walked back to his motorcycle.

"I believe you," Alec said, walking up beside her. "But if they are here, they obviously don't want to be found."

"It's dangerous for us to keep looking," Cole added.

"You're right," Emily sighed. "I'm only out here to save one person, and that's turning into a handful. They know where to find us if they want to be found."

"Exactly," Alec nodded. "We should get moving."

She nodded and turned to walk with Cole back to the SUV.

"Alright, everyone!" Alec yelled. "Let's head out!"

She climbed into the SUV with Cole and closed the door with a sigh. Suddenly, the motorcycle's engine rumble stopped outside her window. She rolled down the window and looked directly at Shawn.

"Next time I say ignore it, fucking ignore it," Shawn spat at her. "None of us are here to die, so you can try to save someone."

"Hey!" Cole yelled beside her. "I don't know what is wrong with you, but you will not talk to her like that."

Shawn said nothing as he pulled forward, taking the caravan's lead.

"I might just beat the snot out of him for fun," Cole said as he put the SUV into drive.

"Well, that confirms it," Emily said, rolling back up the window.

"What's that?" Cole asked, still fuming.

"He knows there was someone there and probably who it was," Emily said. "He was either trying to protect them or...."

"Stop you from walking into an ambush," Cole finished for her.

"Either way," Emily continued. "We are in more danger out here than ever." "Then you need rest," Cole said firmly.

"How can I rest?" Emily asked, surprised.

"Because you have to," Cole answered. "You look like the wind could blow you over. You are so tired. What good are you to us in a fight if you can't keep your damn eyes open?"

Cole did have a point. She was exhausted and knew she wouldn't be able to hold her own right now.

"Just for a bit," Emily insisted.

"I'll wake you when we are getting close," Cole assured her.

She turned and climbed into the backseat as Cole drove. Using her backpack as a pillow, she lay in the bed she had used for months after the flash. It didn't take long for her to fall asleep.

Chapter 9

"Emily," Cole's voice called from the front seat.

"We there?" Emily asked, pulling herself into a sitting position.

"Just about," Cole answered her. "You really think this place will have everything we need?"

"You mean our fake needs," Emily said as she climbed into the front seat. "It has to be better than the one by Sanctuary."

"That place has been picked clean at this point," Cole nodded. "Isn't this where…"

"I found the girls with that pervert," Emily finished.

"Yeah, this is the place. According to the girls, some stores at the end of town were still pretty stocked."

"A one-stop shop," Cole mused.

"That's the plan," Emily nodded. "Quick in and quick out."

"What is that?" Cole said, looking at something on the right side of the highway.

She followed his gaze to the city's welcome sign, or at least that's probably what it used to be. Now the sign was covered with a tarp of some kind with a symbol drawn on it.

She studied the symbol for a moment and recognized that it was the letters "GA." "GA?" Emily said to herself.

"Did someone try to claim this place?" Cole said, looking at her.

"Looks like," Emily nodded. "But why?"

"Definitely not defensible," Cole added. "I'm sure they are long gone by now."

"Yeah," Emily agreed as they continued to drive.

Cole continued down the highway for a few more minutes and followed Shawn off an exit. As the girls said, a cluster of shops and fast-food restaurants was waiting for them. The caravan pulled into the parking lot, and everyone began to climb out of the car.

"I was thinking groups of two," Alec said, walking towards her. "Get what we can in the next few hours and then back on the road." "I agree," Emily said, looking around.

She searched the area around them carefully. While things seemed quiet, the dead were known for coming out of unseen places. She didn't say anything, but something didn't feel right.

"You sure you don't want Shawn to lead this?" Alec said barely above a whisper.

"Not this one," Emily mouthed back.

Alec nodded and walked away, and began putting people into groups. Cole followed, and she assumed he was telling Alec to pair him

with Shawn. She waited patiently for Alec to
assign her a partner.

"You and I are going into the
supercenter," Shawn said beside her.

"I think Alec is still deciding that," Emily
said uncomfortably. It was the first time she felt
uncomfortable with Shawn by her side.

"We need to talk," Shawn said, leaning in
closer.

She looked up at him. He looked cold and
hard at a glance, but she could see the kind man
she had loved trying to break out in his eyes.
She turned her gaze to Alec and Cole, who
watched them a few steps away. Tightening her
grip on her crowbar, she nodded to them and
began to walk with Shawn toward the
supercenter.

Shawn said nothing as they walked and
even kept his distance from her. She stopped as
they reached the doors, and the same symbol
with the GA was painted on them.

"You're on your own in here," Shawn said
to her, looking at the symbol. "Forcing us
together doesn't mean I will protect you."

She tried to hide her confusion at what he
said. He had demanded to come here with her.
She told herself that this had to be just another
act in case whoever he was was trying to protect
her from was watching.

"I'm not any happier about this than you
are," Emily shot back as she opened the door
and walked inside.

She stopped inside the door and opened her mouth to call out for the dead. Shawn suddenly covered her mouth with his hand, lifted her from the ground, and carried her into a small room on the right-hand side. She struggled to break free of the grip but only halfheartedly. She still trusted him and knew that he wouldn't hurt her. Shawn released her once they were in the room and shut the door. She couldn't see anything in the dark, windowless room and remained still. She listened to Shawn rustle around a bit, and then a light burst forth from a flashlight.

"You can't be out here," Shawn said, looking at her with concern.

She could see that his hard exterior was gone, and he was the man she knew once more.

"You couldn't tell me what was happening inside the wall, so I thought out here..." Emily began.

"You thought you would put them all at risk just to get me to talk?!" Shawn growled.

"No," Emily said firmly. "They came up with the plan."

"They know," Shawn said in surprise.

"Everything I do," Emily nodded.

"Shit!" Shawn said, punching a wall.

"Shawn, what is going on?!" Emily pleaded.

"He's going to kill them all," Shawn said, rubbing his hand over his head.

"Who?" Emily asked.

"The General," Shawn replied, still not looking at her. "At least there was no time to let them plan a strategy. We have to get everyone out of here."

"Who is the General?" Emily asked.

"A bad son of a bitch with an army to back it up," Shawn said. "Go out there, tell them we got swarmed by zombies, and I didn't make it. Then get them all out of here."

"You're not coming back?" Emily said, looking at him, confused.

"If I'm not there, they won't have leverage, and you can handle this," Shawn nodded. "I'll fight them on my way out here."

"I'm not leaving you," Emily said firmly. "We will figure this out together."

"That's not an option!" Shawn said, letting his frustration out once more. "For once, could you just do what I say!"

"That's not how this works," Emily reminded him.

"Look…" Shawn began.

"Everyone, back to the cars!" Alec's voice came loud over the radio.

"Fuck," Shawn said, turning and throwing the door open.

She followed him out of the room and looked outside. The once quiet parking area was filled with zombies, all making their way to the caravan.

"Go," Shawn said, opening the door for her.

"Not without you," Emily insisted, looking up at him.

"I'm right behind you," Shawn smiled back at her.

She knew in her heart that he was lying. But the panic she saw outside forced her to walk out the door. She made her way towards the caravan, looking back only once to confirm Shawn had not followed. The entrance to the supercenter was closed, and he was nowhere to be seen. She forced herself to move forward, hitting or stabbing each zombie she saw in the head as she went.

"Emily!" Cole's voice rang out over the walkie. "Where are you?"

Her crowbar and hands were covered in blood as she swung at another zombie. There was no time to reach for the walkie now.

"We have to go, or none of us will make it out," Cole's voice rang out again.

"We're not leaving her!" Rachael's voice came next.

She knew things would be even worse ahead of her if Cole suggested leaving. She stopped trying to make her way to the caravan and instead ran for a shop to her right. She stood on the sidewalk and saw the zombies pouring in. There had to be thousands.

"Shawn!" Rachael's voice came over the walkie. "Where's Emily?"

Shawn didn't answer. She grabbed her walkie from her waist.

"There are too many," Emily said into the walkie. "Get back to Sanctuary."

"No!" Joe screamed. "We're not leaving you again."

"I'll find my way back," Emily smiled to herself. "I always do."

"Emily," Shawn's voice came. "Where are you?"

"Just go," Emily sighed. "I'll be right behind you."

The walkie remained quiet for a few minutes, and the caravan began slowly moving. She breathed a sigh of relief as they pulled out of the parking lot. Her relief was short-lived, though, as the glass in the shop behind her suddenly shattered from a bullet. She ducked and tried to look around for the source. A little closer, and she would have been permanently dead.

She could see that the noise had drawn the dead towards her. She began to run across the storefronts, only stopping behind the brick posts that supported the awning. However, the further she ran, she could see that the dead were coming in from all sides. They had her pinned in with no way of getting out.

Another bullet flew by her hiding post, shattering another window of a furniture store. She knew that with all the stores having glass fronts, she would find no safety here. Her options were only how to die, by bullet or by the zombies.

She closed her eyes and waited for the dead to come. She wouldn't let a sniper without the nerve to look her in the eye be the one to kill her. She felt the hot tears run down her face as she thought of Hope and her family waiting for her when she wouldn't be returning home. She thought of missing Hope growing up and the pain that she would have to endure. The roar of the dead filled her ears, and she knew her time was nearly up.

She opened her eyes and looked at the zombies around her. This had always been her fate to die at the hands of the dead. She had delayed it by being immune, but fate had finally caught up with her. Suddenly, the zombies all began to turn and look at something behind them. She watched as the sea of zombies crashed out of the way, and Shawn came charging through on his motorcycle.

"Get on!" He yelled at her as he stopped a few feet away.

She didn't hesitate and climbed on behind him. Shawn took off once more as she clung to him, trying to keep herself from flying off the back. She laid her face on the soft leather of his vest, the tears still flowing freely.

Shawn sped his way through the streets and stopped at a vet clinic on the edge of town. She released her grip on Shawn and allowed him to help her off the motorcycle. Shawn looked around for a few minutes and pulled a cell phone from his pocket.

"What is that?" Emily asked, confused.

"Be quiet," Shawn instructed her as he pressed a button and then put the phone to his ear.

She heard a voice on the other end, but couldn't understand what they were saying.

"Unable to provide the leader," Shawn said flatly. "She didn't survive the attack."

Shawn listened for a few more minutes, and she looked at him, surprised.

"Negative," Shawn said next. "Received a scratch trying to complete the mission."

She immediately began to look him over. Obviously, he was lying to the voice on the other end. She wasn't dead, and he had no injuries that she could see.

"The General's daughter is alive and well," Shawn said with a look of anger.

She fought every urge to question him on what he was saying.

"Understood," Shawn said to the voice and then hung up the phone.

"Are you alright?" Shawn asked softly as he reached for her.

"What the fuck is going on?" Emily replied as she stepped back from him.

"It's not safe here," Shawn replied. "We have to get moving."

"Who the hell were you talking to?" Emily said as she continued to back away from him.

"There's no time," Shawn replied. "We have to get moving."

She stopped backing away and planted herself on the pavement, crossing her arms.

"They are going to search this whole town for your corpse," Shawn said with a hint of fear in his voice. "If they find you, they will use you just like they used me."

"Who?" Emily repeated.

"I'll explain once you are safe," Shawn assured her.

She looked around and saw that they were exposed where they were. For now, she had to put her complete trust in Shawn. She walked forward and climbed back onto the motorcycle. Shawn climbed in front of her and took off down the road.

She watched as the open green fields and trees passed by them. It wasn't long before she saw they were approaching a small town, even smaller than the one they had just left. She pointed to the grocery store parking lot, signaling for Shawn to pull over. Shawn shook his head no and pointed to the sign above the store. The symbol with the letters "GA" was present once more.

As Shawn continued, she thought of what he said and the symbol. He had mentioned someone called the General and had told her he had an army. Could the symbol mean that the places were controlled by the General's army?

She knew that the bike was too loud to try to ask Shawn now.

Shawn continued to drive down back roads and didn't slow down until the streets turned to dirt. She had tried to keep track of all the twists and turns but found herself completely lost. They drove through a forest and over a creek. Shawn turned once more and slowed the motorcycle after a few minutes. She looked over his shoulder and could see what looked to be a small cabin. Shawn pulled the bike in front of the cabin door and stopped.

She climbed off and watched as Shawn shut off the motorcycle and pulled it around the side of the cabin. When he returned, he opened the cabin's front door and quickly ushered her inside. She remained silent and watched as Shawn walked over to a cabinet and grabbed a few water bottles. She took the one he offered her without a word, but didn't open it. Shawn drank his in a few moments and set the empty bottle back on the counter.

"The water is clean," Shawn assured her. "There's a hand pump outside, so we have plenty."

"What is this place?" Emily asked, looking around.

"It was my grandfather's," Shawn replied. "I used to come here all the time as a kid. It's where I was heading before I met up with Sam and the others."

"We can't stay here," Emily blurted out.

"The dead will tear this place apart."

"There were maybe ten people who lived within five miles of here," Shawn laughed. "There weren't enough living to make the dead a threat."

She stood in shock at how casual he was about the situation. After everything that had happened, he carried on like it was any other day.

"This is where I was going to bring you for our honeymoon," Shawn said as he continued to look around with nostalgia in his eyes.

"Until you called everything off and pushed me away," Emily shot back.

"Yeah," Shawn said, turning his gaze back to her. "Before that."

"Shawn, what is going on?" Emily asked. "And what does it have to do with the General's Army?"

"I'll explain," Shawn said. "But please, sit down and drink some water."

She walked over to the nearest chair and sat down. She quickly took a small sip of water and then returned to Shawn. Shawn took his time sitting down, and the silence hung thick in the air.

"If you're not going to talk, just take me home," Emily finally spoke.

"You can't go home," Shawn replied. "Not yet."

"Why not?!" Emily yelled at him. "You have to tell me what's going on?"

"Our plan worked," Shawn sighed. "They believed we broke up."

"So, you learned what they were up to," Emily said, looking at him.

"It's bigger than we thought," Shawn sighed.

"How big?" Emily asked without hesitation.

"Veronica is the daughter of the General," Shawn explained.

"Who is the General?" Emily asked, frustrated.

"I heard of him when I served," Shawn explained. "He went mad with power, saying the military did not do enough and was run like a joke. He was discharged when it was discovered that he was recruiting soldiers to serve him in his private army."

"And now he's got his army," Emily added.

"He's had the army," Shawn continued. "Now he has a world that he can dominate."

"So, she was gathering supplies for her dad's army," Emily said. "They can't be that much of a problem if they need what we have."

"They don't need it," Shawn said. "They want to hurt other communities by taking what they have so they can be easily conquered."

"So, they want to take over Sanctuary," Emily almost laughed. "If they can find a way in, they might stand a chance."

"You don't understand," Shawn said, shaking his head.

"They do it the same every time. Your family was a part of it without realizing it."
"What?!" Emily asked, confused.

"All those different places they tried to find a home," Shawn continued. "Veronica pushed them to the breaking point by stealing their stuff, telling her dad everything about their inner workings and when to strike."

"And she calls him with the information," Emily said. "So, we get home, find her phone, and destroy it."

"You can't," Shawn said, shaking his head. "Cutting off her communication with him may make things worse. There is only one thing in this world that he actually loves, and that's her."

"Then we use her against him," Emily said, not understanding how this wasn't obvious to Shawn.

"And what about all the innocent people he will kill to get her back?" Shawn asked.

"They are safe behind the wall," Emily said. "He can't get to us."

"Not everyone who needs to be protected is behind the wall!" Shawn said, getting frustrated. "Even if they don't realize they need to be protected."

She sat quietly and looked at Shawn. She was so wrapped up in hearing what he had to say and coming up with a plan, she had overlooked something important. Shawn had a lot of information and was personally involved with the General.

"Who needs to be saved?" Emily asked Shawn.

Shawn looked back at her slowly, not saying a word.

"Who do they have that you need to save?" Emily asked him again.

"He's just a kid," Shawn finally spoke.

"Who?" Emily repeated.

"His name is Dillon," Shawn said. "And he's like my little brother."

Chapter 10

"I met Dillon after I got out," Shawn explained. "He hung around the clubhouse, looking for odd jobs and dreaming of joining one day. I looked after him as best I could. God knows his mom didn't give a damn about him."

"So, you adopted him as a little brother," Emily smiled at him. "That's sweet."

"It wasn't the best place for him to be, but it was better than the streets," Shawn sighed. "I tried to find him after the flash but couldn't. I think that's why I felt so protective when I came across Bobby and his family. It was a chance to save Dillon again."

"How do you know Dillons with him?" Emily asked.

"A few weeks after the breakup, Veronica and Chad came to my apartment," Shawn continued. "They handed me this damn phone with Dillon on the other end. He told me the General would accept me if I agreed to help them into Sanctuary. My job was to weaken your defenses, cause fighting, and learn the code."

"And you agreed," Emily said.

"I wasn't going to do it," Shawn quickly

said. "I pushed you and Hope further away, so I had no chance of learning the code, tried to turn everyone against me, and planned on taking off the first chance I got."

"And do what?" Emily said, frustrated. "Live on the run as long as you could?"

"No," Shawn sighed. "Find a way to get Dillon out."

"How old is he?" Emily asked.

"He'd be seventeen, almost eighteen by now," Shawn replied. "And brainwashed by a madman."

"We'll get him back together," Emily said softly as she took his hand.

"You can't go anywhere near the General," Shawn pleaded. "He will do whatever he has to do to get that code."

"I'm dead," Emily reminded him.

"We have to lay low, so that becomes believable," Shawn replied. "The General doesn't fully trust me. He won't believe it for a while."

"How long do we have to stay here?" Emily asked as the realization of what Shawn said settled in.

"At least a few weeks," Shawn answered. "Months would be better."

"Hope is in danger every day we're gone," Emily blurted out. "She knows the code, and I don't care how old she looks. She's only two."

"Only Julia knows that," Shawn assured her. "They will protect her."

"They will know once Hope opens the gate for the others," Emily pointed out.

"They will protect her," Shawn repeated, trying to calm down.

"I can't...." Emily began.

"You can because it's what's best for her right now," Shawn interrupted.

"So, we just stay here and play house while everything back home falls apart?" Emily said, looking around the cabin.

"We survive so that they can," Shawn said, squeezing her hand.

"How does that thing even work?" Emily said, referring to the cell phone.

"A special chip or something," Shawn replied. "The problem is that it allows all cellphones in a certain range to work when you turn it on."

"That's how my family was able to call," Emily realized.

"Their phones worked because Veronica had hers trying to reach her dad."

"That's what I think," Shawn nodded.

"Is it safe to keep that thing here?" Emily asked. "Can they track it somehow?"

"Only if it's on," Shawn replied. "I turned it off back at the vet clinic."

"You sure?" Emily asked, concerned.

"Yeah," Shawn nodded. "But if it makes you feel better, I'll walk it out into the woods and hide it."

"Why not destroy it?" Emily asked.

"We may need it," Shawn replied. "Best not to destroy any resource until this is over."

Shawn stood from the table and walked out the cabin door. She looked around the small cabin once more. It would have been a great honeymoon spot, but now it was nothing more than her prison. She knew Shawn was right. They had to play out the hand they were dealt. But, yet again, they were going to have to hurt Hope. She was sure the General would tell Veronica she was dead. Hope wouldn't believe it. First, Hope would insist that she would come home. But as more time passed, she would come to believe the lie. She had to trust that her family would keep her safe inside the walls. She was pulled out of her thoughts by Shawn coming back through the door.

"You hungry?" Shawn asked, looking behind him.

"Not really," Emily replied.

"I understand," Shawn nodded. "If you're tired, there's a bed over there, and I'll sleep on the couch."

"With everything I lost today, you're not even going to consider sharing a bed with me?" Emily asked.

"I fucked up," Shawn replied. "A lot. I can't believe that you could ever trust me again. I just want to make sure you and Hope are safe. After that, I'll disappear."

"Like hell, you will!" Emily yelled, standing up. "When will you get it through your thick skull? You're stuck with us for life!"

"You still want me even after all this?" Shawn asked her, confused.

"Even more," Emily said, walking towards him. "Sorry, no easy exit on this one."

"How can you do that?" Shawn said, looking at her with sorrow in his eyes.

"Do what?" Emily asked.

"Still see good in people when they give you no reason to?" Shawn asked.

"It's a character flaw," Emily smiled.

"You are amazing," Shawn smiled at her. "You know that, right?"

"I'm amazing because of the people in my life," Emily replied. "And I'm not letting you get away."

"How do you plan on doing that?" Shawn asked teasingly.

"As soon as we get back, we are getting married," Emily said. "I don't care if everything is burning down around us. We are doing it."

"Yes, ma'am," Shawn said as he pulled her into a hug. "After we get yelled at by Hope, of course."

"Probably," Emily laughed as she lay her head on his chest."

She missed this, being this close to him and feeling safe. For the first time in months, it didn't feel like the world's weight was on her shoulders. Despite everything going on, she felt like everything was how it should be.

"You need to rest," Shawn said to her. "I know you didn't sleep last night."

"I took a nap on the way to town," Emily answered, still refusing to move.

"I'm not going anywhere," Shawn assured her. "You lie down for a bit, and I'll make us something to eat."

"You promise you'll be here when I wake up?" Emily asked, looking up at him.

"I have enough people hunting me," Shawn smiled. "I can't afford to add you to the list."

"I'll find you," Emily teased.

"I know," Shawn grinned. "And I fear you more than any others in that situation."

Shawn released her from the hug and walked her over to the bed. She lay her head on the pillow on top of the old blanket.

"I love you," Emily said as her eyes began to close on their own.

"I love you too," Shawn replied as he kissed her on top of the head. "Get some rest."

She felt the cabin melt away as she fell asleep. Once the cabin was gone, she found herself back in Sanctuary. She ran through the empty streets, searching for Hope. The further she ran without seeing anyone, the more she began to worry. There were no people to be found and not even animals on the farm.

She finally reached the main street and ran into her house.

"Hope!" Emily called out as she ran in. "Marley!"

She ran to each room of the house, finding it empty. She was in a complete panic as she ran back out. She ran around frantically as she reached the street. Suddenly, the gate began to move. She took off, running for it as fast as she could. She knew that Hope was the only one who could open it. She saw no one at the lower control panel, so she took the stairs to the control room. She burst through the door and saw no one.

"Hope!" Emily yelled. "Marley!"

No one answered her, and the gate was opening below her. She ran down the stairs to see who was coming in since there was no one inside. She reached the bottom of the stairs, panting for air.

"Mom?" A grown woman standing in the gate opening said to her.

"Hope?" Emily said to her after studying her for a moment.

"How did you get here?" Hope asked with a look of shock on her face.

"I…" Emily started, unsure how it happened. "Where is everyone? What happened?"

"You died," Hope replied, stepping forward. "They all died."

"What?!" Emily replied, feeling like all of the air was knocked out of her lungs.

"They allow me to come back here every year to pay respects," Hope said as she turned and began to walk between the walls. "Really, it's just to remind me that no one can stand against them."

"Who?" Emily asked as she followed her.

"The General, Chad, and Veronica," Hope said, sounding confused.

Hope stopped walking, and she looked ahead of her. They had reached the small cemetery where there had only been two graves when she was last here. She felt like she had been punched in the gut as she looked at all the graves.

"Other than Veronica and Chad, the General only let the children live," Hope said, looking back at her.

"How did he get in?" Emily asked her.

"I let him in," Hope answered her with tears in her eyes.

"Why?" Emily asked, shocked.

"I saw the motorcycle and thought it was you and Shawn," Hope replied. "You had been gone for months, but I never believed you were dead. We were surrounded, and I knew you would have to hurry."

"So, you opened the gate without being able to see us," Emily said, grabbing Hope by the shoulder. "You did nothing wrong."

"No, I didn't," Hope said, looking angry.

"You did!"

She pulled her hand back in shock.

"You should have been here!" Hope yelled at her. "They all died trying to protect what you built, and you left them!"

"I'm coming back," Emily insisted. "I won't let this happen."

"You already did!" Hope yelled at her. "You were even warned about him!"

Emily was confused and didn't know how to respond.

"Why are you even here?! You should have just stayed dead!"

"You don't mean that," Emily said, trying to hold back tears.

Hope didn't say anything but pushed her hard. She fell backward and into a hole.

"You belong in a grave," Hope said down to her. "Not them."

"Hope!" Emily yelled as Hope began to shovel dirt on top of her.

"Emily!" Shawn yelled, shaking her awake.

Her eyes shot open, and she sat straight up. She looked around the old cabin, remembering that she was taking a nap.

"I can't let them die," Emily said with tears streaming down her face.

"You won't," Shawn assured, wrapping her in a hug. "Is that what you dreamed?"

"All of them," Emily replied. "He didn't want Sanctuary or the supplies. He killed them all, and Hope hated me for it."

"It was just a nightmare," Shawn assured her.

"This whole world is a nightmare!" Emily shot back. "The dead walk around, good people die, but the deranged ones seem stronger than ever!"

"We're stronger," Shawn assured her. "You're stronger."

"I can't mess this up," Emily said, calming herself down.

"I'll help you," Shawn said softly. "We won't mess it up."

She straightened herself and finally began to think clearly.

"You need to eat," Shawn said, standing from the bed and offering her his hand. "I know you haven't eaten today."

"I can't," Emily said, shaking her head no.

"I thought you said we couldn't mess this up?" Shawn asked, not moving. "You starving yourself isn't going to help anyone."

"Fine," Emily replied, taking his hand and forcing herself to stand.

"It's nothing fancy, I promise," Shawn assured her as he led her over to the table.

"Beans," Emily said, looking at the bowls on the table.

"Nothing fancy here," Shawn smiled. "But it will keep us going."

"You may be sleeping on the couch after all," Emily halfheartedly smiled.

"If you eat, I can live with that," Shawn said, pulling out her chair.

She sat down and slowly began to eat the beans. Shawn sat down across from her and started doing the same.

"You know it was just a dream," Shawn said after several minutes.

"I knew that when it started," Emily replied. "But as it went on, it felt so real."

"What happened?" Shawn asked her as they continued to eat.

"It doesn't matter," Emily said, shaking her head. "It was just a dream."

"I know this is hard on you," Shawn said. "But it will all work out."

"We'll make sure it does," Emily replied. She and Shawn finished their food, and Shawn quickly stood to clean up the bowls. She sat quietly and waited for him to finish.

"You said we have to stay out of sight for at least a few weeks," Emily said as Shawn sat back down.

"At least," Shawn replied.

"I just wish there was some way we could let our people know," Emily sighed.

"We can't," Shawn said. "It's too risky."

"I know," Emily defended herself. "It was just a wish."

"It's going to seem like forever," Shawn said, taking her hand. "But soon, we will be home. Hope will be in your arms, and life will be back to normal."

"Tell me more about the General," Emily insisted.

"What do you want to know?" Shawn asked her.

"Everything," Emily replied. "I feel like you're holding something back."

"It's not something I like to talk about," Shawn said. "It's part of the past I want to forget."

"Your past doesn't bother me," Emily assured him. "The more I know, the better prepared I can be for what's to come."

"You won't be going anywhere near him, so it won't help you," Shawn insisted.

"That won't keep him away from me," Emily replied.

"That's my job," Shawn said, standing up.

"You can't protect me from everything," Emily insisted.

"I'm going to make sure none of the dead wander in," Shawn said, walking towards the door.

"You said the chances of the dead finding us were next to nothing," Emily said as he walked out the door.

Shawn didn't stop and slammed the door behind him. She stood up from the table angrily. She knew that Shawn was ashamed of parts of his past, even though she didn't care about his history. She thought about running after him, but decided against it. Instead, she began to navigate the cabin, looking at the pictures on the walls. There were many pictures of a young boy next to an older man. She knew that Shawn was an only child and felt safe assuming it was him with his grandpa. She continued looking at the pictures, smiling at each one as she went along. She stopped in front of Shawn in his military uniform. It was weird for her to see Shawn so clean-cut, almost like he was someone else.

"That was the last time I saw him," Shawn said suddenly behind her. "He passed away while I was overseas."

"I'm sorry," Emily said, looking at him. "But it looks like he was proud of you."

"He was," Shawn said, looking at the pictures. "He would have tanned my hide if he saw what I did when I got out."

"Not much into motorcycles?" Emily asked.

"No, he rode when he was younger," Shawn replied. "It was the club he would have had a problem with."

"He loved you," Emily assured him. "I can see that in these pictures."

"He was the only father I ever knew," Shawn said, looking at the pictures. "He would have loved you, though."

"Really?" Emily smiled.

"Oh, yeah," Shawn smiled. "My grandma was a lot like you, and he was with her for over sixty years. Always said she was better than he deserved."

"Sounds like you both had something in common," Emily smiled.

"I'm sorry I left like that," Shawn said, looking back at her.

"I know you don't like talking about your past," Emily nodded. "We got weeks for you to fill me in."

"But you're not going to wait that long," Shawn smiled at her. "You simply can't help yourself."

"You don't know that," Emily said, faking being insulted.

"I know you," Shawn smiled. "But can you at least give me until tomorrow?"

"I think I can wait that long," Emily smiled back.

Chapter 11

Shawn didn't bring up the topic of the General the next day, and she didn't push. He kept the conversations light and friendly. He went out three times a day and checked for the dead, or at least that's what he told her. She knew he was making sure they had not been found and was avoiding talking about the General. Two weeks passed, and she didn't push. However, the time had come to discuss going home. She waited until Shawn returned from his morning perimeter check to talk to him.

"I think we should take some of these pictures back with us," Emily said, looking at the photos.

"Grandpa wouldn't mind," Shawn said casually. "We'll pack them up when we are ready to go."

"When are we planning to head out?" Emily asked as innocently as she could.

"Soon," Shawn answered, not meeting her gaze.

She felt herself get frustrated at how vague he was being.

"It's time we went home," Emily said, stepping in front of him.

"You're right," Shawn sighed. "Get your stuff together, and I'll get you home."

"We will get home," Emily replied, realizing he had changed the wording.

"I can't go back without Dillon," Shawn said, walking away. "I can't get him away from the General inside those walls."

"What is the deal with this guy?" Emily blurted out. "You said you would tell me."

"I know," Shawn sighed. "And I hoped you had given up on it."

"You know me better than that," Emily said firmly.

"Fine," Shawn said, sitting on the edge of the bed. "What do you want to know?"

"Everything," Emily replied, sitting next to him.

"I told you, I heard about him while serving," Shawn started. "When I got out, and things were rough, he found me. He offered me a position in his army."

"And you turned him down," Emily said, encouraging him to keep talking.

"He isn't the kind of guy who takes no for an answer," Shawn continued. "He and his guys hounded me for nearly a year until I joined the club."

"How did they hound you?" Emily asked, knowing he was holding something back.

"If I hadn't joined the club and kept saying no, I would have been killed," Shawn blurted out. "I can hold my own, but this guy had a literal fucking army!"

"What was the point of it?" Emily asked. "What did he want you to do?"

"What I do for you," Shawn said, looking at her. "Organize security and keep the guys in line."

"But why?" Emily asked.

"He was preparing for this world," Shawn laughed. "He kept saying everything would fall, and he would be the one to set it right. I thought he was just fucking nuts. Once I was in the club, he left me alone. I forgot about him until that phone call."

"And you're sure it was Dillon on the other end?" Emily asked.

"As sure as I can be," Shawn replied. "He was only fourteen the last time I talked to him."

"Alright," Emily said, realizing she was pushing him too far. "So, how do we get him back?"

"I know where they are, and I can get in," Shawn replied. "We must keep daddy's little girl from tipping them off."

"How do you plan on doing that out here?" Emily asked.

"I don't know," Shawn sighed. "But I can't let that bitch know I'm alive."

"You said she talks to her dad," Emily began to think. "Checks in with him?"

"Yeah," Shawn nodded. "Once a week."

"That's why we had to let everyone believe we were dead for at least a few weeks," Emily said, suddenly realizing the plan.

"Yeah," Shawn nodded. "But I have no idea how to work things now."

"Go get the phone," Emily said. "I know how."

Shawn looked at her, confused, and did not move.

"Hope keeps my old phone charged," She explained. "She likes to look at the photos and listen to the old voicemails. I can leave her a message and tell her to play it for the others."

"What would you say?" Shawn asked, still doubting her plan.

"I don't know," Emily admitted. "For them to lock them both up until we get there."

"But if she misses her check-in, there will be an army between Sanctuary and us," Shawn pointed out.

"Right," Emily sighed, thinking again. "They could promote them." "What?"

Shawn asked, confused.

"You know they are still holding on to hope that we are out here," Emily said, getting excited. "Tell them to hold a memorial and name Chad and Veronica the new leaders. They will be so busy; they will never see us coming."

"But if the gates open, she is going to grab that phone, and it's all over," Shawn interrupted.

"Then we go in while she's sleeping," Emily smiled. "You know she won't get out of bed for anything."

"It's risky," Shawn said, shaking his head.

"We have to get into Sanctuary to get the help we need to save Dillon," Emily argued. "Otherwise, it's just me and you against an army. Which is riskier?"

"I wasn't going to let you go with me," Shawn admitted, looking at the floor."

"You think I was going to sit here and let you go by yourself?" Emily sighed.

"Of course not," Shawn said, running his hand through his hair. "It's part of what I have been trying to figure out these past few weeks. How to get you busy doing something else so I could slip away and handle this."

"Not going to happen," Emily said firmly.

"Why?" Shawn asked, looking at her with pain and anger in his eyes.

"Because I love you," Emily said, surprised.

"I don't get it," Shawn said, standing up. "I wasn't a good guy. Hell, my past is already biting you in the ass. Why would you want to love someone like me?"

"I didn't know you before," Emily admitted. "But I know the man who held my hand and cared for me after my daughter was born. The guy he ran in and saved me from Jeff the night Marley was shot. Without a second thought, the man who would die to save my daughter or me."

"Yeah, but," Shawn began.

"No," Emily interrupted. "From the moment I met you, you have been nothing but a kind, loving, protective pain in my ass! You are the man I could have only dreamed of falling in love with."

Shawn said nothing and just stood staring at her.

"Now, you have a choice to make," Emily continued. "We either go home and get help to save Dillon, or you and I go in together. Either way, let's get this over with so we can go home to our daughter and family."

"Alright," Shawn nodded. "I'll go get the phone."

You'd better come back," Emily called after him. "Otherwise, I will find the General, rescue you and Dillon, and kick your ass back at Sanctuary."

"I know," Shawn smiled. "I'll be back." She watched as he walked out the door. She watched the door, each second feeling like an eternity waiting for Shawn to walk back through it. Suddenly, Shawn burst through the door, and she could see the fear and panic on his face.

"Take the phone," Shawn said, shoving it into her hands. "Stay in here and be quiet."

"What's going on?" Emily asked, grabbing his arm.

"We're not alone," Shawn said, looking at the door. "I'll lead them away, and you find a way back home."

"No," Emily insisted. "We are in this together."

"They will kill you on sight," Shawn said hurriedly. "They want me alive. It's our only shot."

"I'm not losing you again," Emily insisted, pulling at his arm.

"You won't," Shawn said softly, pulling her close. "Take this."

She watched as Shawn pulled a chain from around his neck and handed it to her.

"I don't understand," Emily said, taking the chain and looking at the ring that hung from it.

"It will keep you safe," Shawn insisted. "Now, wait until dark and head back to Sanctuary.

"There were so many turns," Emily said, putting the chain around her neck.

"I did that to ensure we weren't followed," Shawn explained. "Just follow the road out and make a left when it ends. When you reach the pavement, make a right and follow it back to Ozark. You know your way home from there."

Shawn pulled away and took her hand. She looked to see him pushing keys into her hand.

"Go slow until you are on pavement," Shawn said, closing her hand around the keys.

"Where are they taking you?" Emily asked, looking back at him.

"Their compound," Shawn replied. "All the information I have is in my apartment."

"Where'd he go?!" a voice rang outside the cabin.

"Shit," Shawn breathed, looking toward the voice.

"Shawn," Emily said, following his gaze, not trying to hide the fear in her voice.

"I love you," Shawn said, kissing her.

"I love you too," Emily replied with tears.

Shawn made his way across the cabin without another word and walked out the door. "I'm right here!" Shawn called out to the unknown voice.

"You didn't check in," an angry male voice replied.

"Lost the phone," Shawn said quickly.

"Where's the bitch?" the voice asked, just as angry.

"Buried out back," Shawn replied casually.

"He wanted the body," the voice replied.

"I agreed to kill her," Shawn said with anger. "But she deserved to be buried."

"You'll pay for that decision," the voice almost laughed.

"Where's Dillon?" Shawn asked.

"Back at the compound," the voice continued to laugh.

She realized that it must have been Dillon who told them about the cabin, about where Shawn could be.

"Why didn't he come?" Shawn asked, confused.

"He probably would have if he knew you were alive," the voice replied.

"I talked to him," Shawn said, confused. "He knows."

"He knows the General agreed to look for you," the voice replied. "Took him a while to remember where this place was, so we could check it out."

"You son of a bitch," Shawn said with anger.

"Yeah," the voice laughed. "Aren't we all? Let's get moving."

She had made herself as small as possible next to the bed. She made sure she was out of view of the windows as the sounds of footsteps moved around the outside of the cabin. After a few minutes, she did not relax. She stayed in her hiding spot and waited.

Several hours passed, and she saw that the sun was beginning to set. She stood up, grabbed a backpack, and made her way to the wall of pictures. She quickly pulled several pictures off the wall and put them into the bag. She then grabbed a pistol from the footlocker and an ammo box. Once she felt she was ready

to go, she pulled out the cell phone and dialed
her old phone number. She wasn't surprised that
the phone went to voicemail, and she listened to
her voice recording.

"Hope, I'm so sorry. I'm fine, and so is
Daddy. I'm on my way home, but I need you to
play this message for our family." Emily began.

"I'm coming back tonight," Emily said
after swallowing hard. "Chad and Veronica can
not be near the gate until dawn. Do whatever it
takes to keep them away, but do not arrest them.
Make them think they are in charge now if you
have to. I'll explain when I get home, but my
coming back has to be a secret, or Shawn could
die."

She struggled to continue after saying
that Shawn could die out loud.

"The sun is getting ready to set now,"
Emily continued. "It will take me a few hours,
but I'm on my way. Hope, I love you."

She hung up the phone, quickly powered
it off, and put it into the backpack. She put the
bag on and made her way outside. She found the
motorcycle still hidden beside the cabin. She
struggled to push it from the hiding spot. It was
heavier than she thought, the way Shawn moved
it around.

It took her several minutes, but soon she
could get on it and start it up. Shawn had given
her a few short lessons, all of which went
horribly wrong. She knew that she would have
to figure it out now. She put the motorcycle in

gear and slowly began to drive down the dirt road. She continued slowly as she made the first turn. The sun was well into setting, and she knew she would lose the light soon. However, she dared not go any faster until she reached the pavement.

She breathed a sigh of relief as she made the right turn and began accelerating. By the time she reached the vet clinic, she was driving by the light of the headlights. She prayed that Hope had gotten her message, and she sped along the road. She made her way back to the highway and continued on her way. She expected herself to cry as she drove, but no tears came. Instead, her body filled with rage and determination. She would get Shawn back, and all those who caused this would pay.

She knew it was after midnight when she finally reached the logging road. She drove the motorcycle slowly up the street until she could barely make out the wall. She shut off the bike and began to push it the rest of the way.

"Thank God!" Alec exclaimed as he walked out of the tree line towards her.

"Don't give thanks just yet," Emily said as she continued to push the motorcycle. "This is just starting."

"What happened?" Alec asked, grabbing the motorcycle and pushing it. "Where's Shawn?"

"They took him," Emily said, staring ahead at the gate. "But I'm going to get him back."

Alec said nothing else as they walked towards the gate. She entered the code and opened the gate just enough for them to get in.

"Put it by the graves," Emily instructed once they were inside.

Alec nodded and pushed the motorcycle where she had told him.

"Everyone's waiting for you in the quarantine cabins," Alec said as he walked away.

She turned and headed in the opposite direction. Once inside, she could hear voices coming from the first cabin. She opened the door, and all of the voices fell silent.

"It's just me," Emily said as she stepped inside.

"Mommy!" Hope exclaimed as she ran towards Emily.

She smiled as she scooped up Hope and held her in a hug.

"You got my message," Emily said barely above a whisper into Hope's ear.

"How did you do that?" Hope asked, confused.

"I'll explain when Alec gets here," Emily replied, setting her down. "He's hiding the motorcycle by the graves."

No one asked questions; each hugged her and told her they were glad she was alright. It wasn't long before Alec joined them in the small cabin.

"What were you doing outside?" Emily asked when she saw him.

"We didn't know if you were hurt or what," Alec began. "I thought it best if someone was waiting for you."

"He insisted," Sam spoke up.

"Thank you," Emily smiled at Alec as she hugged him. "I'm sorry, I was a little short. It's been a long day."

"It's been a long two weeks," Charlie corrected her. "What happened out there?"

She sighed and began to explain everything to them. She explained about Veronica and the General, how the cell phones worked, and Dillon. She found it difficult to tell them about Shawn being taken to the compound. Everyone sat in silence, even after she finished explaining.

"I'm getting him back," Emily said confidently to break the silence.

"Where is this place?" Joe asked.

"I don't know," Emily admitted. "Shawn said all his information on it was in his apartment."

"I can look for it," Joe nodded. "No one will find me out of place in the apartments."

"Where are Chad and Veronica?" Emily asked.

"In your house," Christine answered. "They moved in a week ago."

"They are back together and claiming to be in charge because he's Hope's father," Sarah said through gritted teeth.

"She's been staying with us at the farm," Jacob said.

"They really let her leave?" Emily said in surprise.

"They don't know," Hope said, looking sad. "I ran away and have been hiding from them. All they want from me is the gate code. They said you were dead, and they would kill me if I didn't give it to them."

"We were actually going to take them out tonight, but Hope got your message," Julia said. "We will handle them in the morning," Emily assured them.

She looked around and suddenly realized who was missing.

"Where's Marley?" Emily asked.

"He's fine," Hope assured her. "He's hiding."

"They insisted he had gone completely crazy without you," Cole said, shaking his head. "They wanted us to put him down."

"What!?" Emily snarled.

"He's been hiding in the shop for a while now," Cole continued. "I can get him here tonight. I just wanted to ensure you made it before moving him."

"I'd appreciate that," Emily nodded.

"We may have another problem," Sam said, not looking up.

"What?" Emily asked.

"There is a small group of people who have sided with Veronica and Chad," Sam continued. "Turns out they have been recruiting since they arrived here."

"Do we know who they are?" Emily asked.

"Yeah," Sam nodded. "And they will cause a fuss if we do anything to Chad or Veronica."

"Then we lock them all up until I have time to deal with this," Emily said without hesitation.

Chapter 12

She sat in the cabin that night. Hope slept on the bed, and Marley stretched out before the door. She knew she wouldn't sleep and didn't even try to lie down. It had only been a few hours since everyone had left, but it felt much longer to her. A soft knock on the door made her jump.

"It's me," Joe whispered into her.

"I'll come out," Emily whispered back as she stood and walked towards the door.

Marley stood and waited for her to open the door. She knew he wouldn't let her go anywhere without him now. She opened the door and walked outside to where Joe was waiting.

"Did you find it?" Emily asked, closing the door behind Marley.

"Yeah," Joe said, handing her a few sheets of paper. "Took a while, but he was clever."

She looked at the papers and saw the drawings that Hope had made for Shawn. She knew they were the ones that had hung on the apartment refrigerator.

"On the back," Joe said to her. "He left them in plain sight."

She turned over the pictures and recognized the handwriting as Shawn's. He had written down every conversation with Chad, Veronica, or whoever he believed to be Dillon. She read through each quickly, looking for any clue about where the compound was.

"It's a lot," Joe said, pointing at the papers. "They never say exactly where, but he puts the compound's location here."

She looked to where Joe was pointing at the paper.

"That's hours away," Emily breathed.

"And in the opposite direction than our groups normally go," Joe added.

"We don't know if it's her day to check in," Emily sighed. "If we take too long to get there after they are locked up, they could be on to us."

"It's a risk," Joe nodded. "But I still think we would have the upper hand."

"We can't mess this up," Emily sighed.

"We won't," Joe assured her. "We will get him back."

"Yeah," Emily nodded.

"Everyone's ready to move now," Joe replied. "Ready to come back from the dead?" "Let's do this," Emily nodded.

"I'm coming to," Hope said from the doorway.

"I'm not sure…." Emily began.

"Don't bother," Joe interrupted Emily. "She's just as stubborn as you are."

"Just stay close to Marley and me,"
Emily conceded.

"Yes, ma'am," Hope nodded, walking
closer.

"The others are in a position to arrest the
supporters," Joe said calmly. "Cole and Jacob
are waiting outside your house to back you up
with Veronica and Chad."

"Let's do this," Emily nodded.

They all walked towards the door and
made their way into Sanctuary. The streets were
silent and dark. The sun would rise within the
hour, but they were shielded by the darkness for
now. She walked towards her house, where
Jacob and Sam were waiting on the porch.

"Doors unlocked," Sam said softly.

"Stay behind me," Emily said to Hope as
she opened the door.

Hope listened and stepped behind her
once they were inside.

"Where does Steven sleep?" Emily asked
Hope softly.

"My room," Hope replied.

"Can you go to him and make sure he
stays there?" Emily asked.

"Yes, ma'am," Hope nodded.

Emily led the group up the stairs and
stopped outside her bedroom door. She watched
as Hope went to the bedroom and shut the door
behind herself. She breathed a little easier now,
knowing that both kids would be protected from
what was happening. She looked around at the

others before turning the doorknob and throwing the door open. Chad and Veronica sat up straight as the door hit the wall.

"What the fuck?!" Chad yelled, looking around.

"Honey," Emily smiled at him. "I'm home."

"You're dead!" Veronica yelled back as she turned to reach for something.

Emily ran across the room and grabbed the phone from her hand.

"Daddy can't save you now," Emily smiled as she took the phone.

"You have no idea what you are doing!" Veronica spat at Emily.

"Let's see if I got the whole story," Emily began. "Your dad is 'The General," and he has been bat shit crazy since before the flash. He put together a private army because he believed the world would fall one day and only he could rebuild it, as he believed was the right way."
"How…" Veronica began.

"Not done," Emily interrupted. "After the flash, he gave you one of these nifty phones that continues to work with the unfortunate side effect of making all phones within a certain radius work. But you must use the phone to check in once a week and give Daddy information on other existing settlements. He then comes in, killing all the survivors and taking their supplies with only you and my family escaping, to find another group and turn them over as well."

She could see that Veronica was beginning to panic and continued.

"When you told your dad about Shawn, he used Dillon against Shawn to give you the edge you needed to take down this place. Hope would give you the code if I were dead, and you could just let the army come in and take it all." "It worked," Veronica blurted out. "Shawn did as he was told."

"Then how am I still alive?" Emily sneered, leaning closer to Veronica.

Veronica was white as a ghost at this point. Having all of her secrets exposed was something she was not ready for.

"You know I have to check in," Veronica said, finally finding the courage to speak. "If I don't he …."

"He won't have to come here," Emily interrupted. "I'm going to bring the fight to him."

"He'll kill you," Chad finally spoke.

"Or I'll kill him," Emily smiled. "Now, get the fuck out of my house."

Cole grabbed Chad by the arm and pulled him out of bed. She did the same with Veronica and tied her hands behind her back.

"Put them in the cells," Emily said as Sam took Veronica.

"You think everyone is going to stand with you?" Veronica said, trying to get away from Sam.

"Your followers will be waiting for you," Emily replied.

"What about our son?" Chad yelled as he reached the door.

"He'll be taken care of," Emily replied. "He doesn't deserve to suffer because you two are his parents."

"You can't do this!" Veronica yelled.

"I just did!" Emily yelled back.

She felt stronger as Chad and Veronica were dragged out of the house.

"Mommy," Hope said from the doorway. "Steven is hurt."

"What?!" Emily said as she ran into the bedroom.

The boy was lying on the bed, and even across the room, she could see he was in bad shape. His face was swollen and bruised, and streaks of blood were dried on his face.

"Grab my walkie and tell Doc to meet us at the clinic," Emily instructed Hope as she picked up Steven.

"Doc," Hope said into the walkie. "Meet us at the clinic."

With Marley behind, she was already running down the stairs with Steven before Hope could finish. She ran out the open door and into the street. Doc was already waiting for them in front of the clinic.

"What happened?!" Doc yelled as he came running towards her.

"We found him in bed like this," Emily replied as she ran with Doc to the clinic.

Steven lay still and quiet in her arms as she laid him on the bed. Doc quickly set to work examining and helping Steven. She stood with Hope and Marley in silence and watched.

"He'll live," Doc said after several minutes. "It's too early to tell if he will have permanent damage. They really did a number on him."

"You're saying they beat him," Emily said with anger and disgust.

"And for quite a while," Doc replied. "The oldest injuries are to places we wouldn't be able to see."

"Hope, stay with Steven," Emily ordered the little girl as she walked out of the clinic.

She didn't need to glance back to know Hope had stayed, but Marley was right behind her. She quickly made her way to the security building and saw they were still fighting to get Chad and Veronica into a cell.

"Leave them," Emily said as she continued to walk.

"What's going on?" Cole asked as he looked at her, still holding Chad.

She swung as hard as she could and hit Chad in the face. Cole let go of Chad and allowed him to fall to the ground. She stood over Chad and continued beating him as hard as possible.

"Stop it!" Veronica screamed.

She stopped hitting Chad, stood, and swung at Veronica. Chad attempted to stand up, probably in an attempt to stop Emily. But Marley jumped on his chest and bared his teeth, inches from Chad's face. After striking Veronica several times, she finally stepped back from the two of them. Marley slowly backed off from Chad and joined Emily.

"Now you know how he felt!" Emily screamed at the two of them. "He did nothing, and you beat the shit out of him just because you could!"

"He's our son!" Chad yelled back at her. "It's none of your business!"

"I should fucking kill you!" Emily screamed, stepping forward. "And I still might! Get the fuck in the cell, and don't say another God damn word!"

Chad and Veronica helped each other into the cell and sat in silence.

"Is the boy alright?" Cole asked as they all gathered around her.

"Doc says he'll live, but we can't know if there's permanent damage or not," Emily replied, still breathing heavily with anger.

"We didn't know," Jacob said with rage in his eyes.

"It's not our fault," Emily replied. "We will make sure they never touch him again."

"We should…" Alec began.

"We don't have time," Emily interrupted. Our clock started running the moment I opened that door."

"I'll get everyone together," Sarah said as she ran out of the room.

Moments later, she heard the announcement over the loudspeakers.

"I can't," Emily breathed, her fists still clenched, stained with Chad and Veronica's blood.

"We'll handle it," Sam assured her as he walked towards the door.

She thought about looking at the other faces in the cells, but decided against it. She wasn't ready to know who supported Chad and Veronica. She could hear Sam outside explaining what they had done that night and that Shawn was taken captive.

"What about Emily?!" Someone yelled from the crowd.

"I'm here," Emily said, stepping out of the doorway.

"Where have you been?!" someone yelled.

"Why don't we just stay here and hide?!" someone else yelled.

"They said you were dead!" another voice added.

"I'm not asking anyone to go," Emily replied. "I had to let them believe I was dead. Otherwise, they would have killed all of you to get to me."

Sam stepped aside and let her address the crowd, seeing she had found her strength to talk to them.

"I am going back out," Emily continued. "I will get Shawn back, just as I would for any of you. If you want to come, I will accept the help. If you think it's better to stay here, I'm fine with that too."

"Why were people taken from their homes?!" another voice yelled.

"We took the people known to side with Chad and Veronica," Emily answered. "I was not willing to risk letting people run free in our town that supported child beaters and people who planned on killing everyone here for our supplies."

"What if they didn't know?!" the same voice yelled. "They could be innocent!" "They could," Emily agreed. "But I don't have time to sort out who is and isn't. If it means protecting all of you, I will lock them up until I can ensure they're safe."

"What gives you the right to make that decision?!"

"You did," Emily replied angrily. "You did when you signed the ledger and trusted me to enforce the rules and protect every one of you. Something I am willing to die for if needed. I will not apologize for protecting you. I will not apologize for calling each of you family and wanting to know that you are safe!"

There were some grumbles through the crowd that she couldn't make out.

"There is no time to argue or debate," Emily said firmly. "I am leaving to save one of our own. When I return, there is a good chance the enemy won't be far behind me, ready and willing to kill every last one of us. If you aren't willing to take a stand and fight with us, then you are free to go. The gate will open for all who wish to leave at dawn."

"And if we chose to stay?" Rachael's voice called out.

"Then be ready to defend what we have built here," Emily answered. "Margaret and Sarah will be left in charge of organizing our defense and making sure everyone is prepared."

"And if you don't make it back this time?!" a voice called out.

"Julia will ensure things keep going until Hope is old enough," Emily replied. "But everyone will need to work together, or Sanctuary will fall."

With that, she turned and headed back inside the security building.

"Quite a speech," Sam said as he followed her, closing the door.

"Just the truth," Emily replied. "I plan on leaving in just a few minutes."

"Everyone is gathered by the front gate and ready to go," Sam assured her.

"I'll take Shawn's motorcycle," Emily said as she looked at him.

"Alec fueled it up, and it's ready," Sam nodded. "You go see Hope, and we'll be waiting when you're ready."

She said nothing as she nodded and walked towards the door. The crowd was gathered around Margaret and Howard, who were giving directions. She and Marley made their way to the clinic and found Hope sitting with Steven. She fought back the tears as she looked at the boy lying in bed.

"Doc says he'll be asleep for a while," Hope said to her.

"He needs a lot of rest to heal," Emily assured her.

"You're leaving to save Daddy," Hope said calmly.

"I am," Emily nodded.

"And you want me to stay here," Hope said, still not looking at her.

"Yes," Emily admitted. "I need you to take care of Steven."

"Yes, ma'am," Hope said coldly.

"Do you want me to stay?" Emily asked, kneeling beside Hope's chair.

"I want you to bring Daddy home," Hope said, looking at her with tears. "I want us all to be safe and bad people to stop hurting us."

"Me too," Emily said, wiping her tears. "But sometimes, the good things in life are the things you have to fight to keep."

"You fight the monsters outside," Hope said as she hugged her. "I'll make sure we're ready here."

"I love you, kiddo," Emily said as she hugged Hope.

"I love you too, Mommy," Hope said, hugging her back.

She hugged Hope for a few more minutes and then forced herself to stand up.

"No goodbyes," Hope said, turning back to Steven. "I'll see you in a few hours."

"I'll see you in a few hours," Emily replied as she walked out of the clinic with Marley.

"I'll take care of them," Julia said as she stepped outside.

"I know," Emily nodded, wiping away a few stray tears. "Thank you."

"Not needed," Julia assured her. "Now go get our biker man back."

She nodded and walked towards the gate. Everyone was already in their vehicles and ready to go. She entered the code and started the motorcycle. She followed everyone outside the gate and entered the code to close it.

"Emily!" Joe yelled from inside the SUV.

"Yeah," Emily said as she walked toward him.

"Thought you might need these," Joe said, handing her weapons out of the window. "I added shoulder straps so you could carry them while you ride."

"Thanks," Emily said, looking at the crowbar and the shotgun.

"I put extra ammo in your bag with the handgun," Joe replied.

"Marley will need to ride with you," Emily said as she reached for the back door of the SUV."

Marley climbed inside with Christine and Charlie. She quickly closed the door behind him and stepped back.

"We'd better get moving," Emily said as she slung the weapons onto her back.

She climbed onto the motorcycle and drove to the front of the line of cars. She hadn't had time to see who had come with her and didn't plan on taking it. Even if they all turned around, she wasn't coming home without Shawn.

She led all the cars onto the main road and turned right. Everything they had scavenged and explored had been to the left. They had gone about a mile in this direction when setting up the pits, but no further. She drove the motorcycle faster than she was comfortable with down the paved road. She wanted to put as much distance between them and Sanctuary before dawn. She continued to drive as the sun rose, and their caravan could be seen on the road. The sun had been up for about an hour as she began to make the turns to the compound location. She began to slow her pace as they neared the location. She caught sight of what could have been a guard tower in the distance and pulled over.

"We close?" Cole asked as everyone got out of the cars.

"I think so," Emily nodded. "It will be best to walk from here."

"Stealth?" Joe asked, joining them.

"If they are half as strong as Veronica seems to think, we don't stand a chance of just charging in," Emily replied. "If any of you want to go back, now's the time."

"Lead the way," Alec replied, holding a rifle.

She turned with Marley and began to lead them all towards the compound. Despite not knowing what she was heading into, she felt no fear. She was determined to get Shawn back, and nothing was going to stop her.

Chapter 13

Emily and the others made their way slowly through the trees towards the compound. She glanced down occasionally to see that Marley was on high alert, scanning the area around them. They traveled for about an hour before she stopped. The guard tower she had spotted was in clear view. She could only pray that the trees overhead provided enough cover to hide them from whoever was up there.

She watched the tower for several minutes and felt confident that there was only one person up there. From this distance, she could see very little about him. He was dressed in a military camouflage uniform. She couldn't be positive but thought he looked young, maybe in his late teens. She couldn't help but wonder if she might be looking at Dillon and not even know it.

She turned her focus to the tower. A wooden wall was built behind it. While it was not nearly as tall or secure as Sanctuary's, it looked strong. She couldn't see it having any significant weaknesses like Jeff's had with the truck door.

"Maybe we pose as people looking for a

place," Sam suggested. "Give them a chance to recruit us to get inside."

"The General is very picky about who he takes in," Emily replied. "He prefers to kill most people and take what they have."

"So, we'd be lucky if one of us got in," Sam sighed.

"They probably have descriptions on all of us," Cole spoke up. "Who knows how much Veronica told them?"

"We will have to find another way in," Emily said.

Suddenly, Marley began to let out a low growl. She immediately turned her attention to him. She had heard that growl before when they were in danger. Marley was glaring toward the road they had just come from. She followed his gaze and tried her best to see what he saw. The trees and underbrush provided the cover she had hoped for, but hid the danger from her.

"Someone's here," Emily whispered as she finally saw movement.

"Maybe they're trying to sneak in like us," Joe said hopefully.

"Or maybe they are watching the perimeter for people like us," Emily replied. "We need to split up."

"No!" Charlie insisted. "We stand a better chance if we stay together."

"A better chance of all of us getting caught!" Emily replied. "We will all leave here together, I promise. But for now, we all have to survive to get inside."

She quickly divided them up into groups and sent them in different directions. Within moments, she stood alone with only Marley, Cole, Sam, Alec, and Jacob.

"You four head that way," Emily instructed them.

"What about you?" Alec asked, not moving.

"It's too dangerous for me to be found with any of you," Emily insisted. "We'll be fine."

"We're not leaving you alone!" Cole insisted.

"No one's leaving," a gruff voice suddenly spoke.

She turned to see a large man standing beside her. Marley lowered his head and began to bare his teeth.

"What do we have here?" the man asked, looking at them.

She didn't respond and found herself staring at the man. He had something familiar, but she couldn't put her finger on it.

"Forget how to speak, love?" the gruff voice asked, stepping closer to her.

She shuddered at being called love again. The thought of Jeff ran through her mind, but she was optimistic that this man had not been there.

"We're lost," Emily blurted out.

"I doubt that," the man laughed, looking at his friends.

Her eyes immediately fell on the symbol on his back. He was wearing a leather vest with the same symbol that Shawn wore. He said it was part of their club and showed they were members. Her eyes darted to the others he was with, each wearing a leather vest. She wasn't sure if she should feel relief or fear this discovery. Shawn had said that his brothers did things he couldn't do, which he knew were wrong. But their bond had been strong, and they were willing to die for each other.

"One of our group was taken," Emily blurted out. "We're here to get him back."

"You came here for one person," the man smiled, leaning close to her face. "You are a brave little bird."

"I'd die for him," Emily said back firmly.

"Every woman says that little bird," the man sneered. "But there are few who mean it. You're probably just another bitch in heat thinking you're tough."

She felt a rage boil up inside her that she could not control. She reached up and smacked the man as hard as she could. His face felt like stone under her hand, causing pain to shoot from her hand up her arm. She didn't cry out in pain, though; she instead stared the man in the eye.

"You will not call me that!" Emily said forcefully back to the man.

"You little…" the man began as he reached for her.

"Wait!" another man yelled as he stepped in between. "Where did you get that?"

She looked to see what he was pointing to. She looked down at Shawn's ring that hung on a chain around her neck.

"It belongs to a real man," Emily said, looking back at the man.

"You got it from a living man?" the man asked. "Not off the dead."

"He's the one I'm here to get back," Emily said more softly.

"We take them all back," the man said, turning back to the man she slapped. "Clint will want to talk to her."

"I'm not going anywhere!" Emily shot back.

"You are," the man said, not looking at her. "And I suggest you don't harm her."

"Give me one good reason why not!" the angry man yelled. "Someone needs to put this bitch in line!"

"Do as you wish," the man said, holding up his hands. "But you can tell Clint why you decided to put your hands on Shawn's old lady."

"He hasn't been seen in years!" the man angrily replied.

"Doesn't matter," the man said, beginning to walk away. "The club is for life." "Shit!" the man said as he grabbed her.

"What about my friends?" Emily asked, fighting against his pull.

"They come too," the man said, still not turning back. "Control the dog, or we'll bury him here."

She looked back at the others and saw them each getting their own escort, two for Alec. She knew that fighting this would only get all of them killed.

"Easy, boy," Emily said to Marley as the man began to drag her back the way they came.

Marley stopped baring his teeth and followed, but was still ready to attack at a moment's notice. The men led them back to the road where they had left the vehicles.

"What's the plan now, Will?" the man holding on to Emily asked angrily. "We're supposed to let them all ride bitch back to camp. The big guy will never fit."

"Blindfold them and put them in the SUV," Will replied.

"And who's expected to leave their ride behind?" the man asked, even more agitated.

"I will," Will replied calmly.

"You can't..." the angry man began.

"You tell me one more time what I can and can't do, and we will have a problem, Billy!" Will shot back.

She didn't know much about how the club worked, but she felt that Will outranked Billy. Billy grumbled as he pulled a bandana from his pocket and tied it around her eyes. She then felt him pull at her arm and found herself being stuffed into the SUV. Based on sound, the others soon joined her.

"Call the dog," Will's voice rang out. "Unless you want him to stay here."

"Marley!" Emily called out. She heard the large dog jump into the SUV.

Moments later, someone else climbed into the SUV beside her and started it.

"It's not far," Will's voice rang out. "And will be a warmer welcome than those commandos would have given you."

She said nothing and sat silent as the SUV began to drive down the road. The others in the back seat remained silent as if following her lead. She tried her best to pay attention to Will's turns but soon had no idea how to make her way back to the compound. She was still searching for a plan as the SUV stopped.

"You're supposed to hand over trespassers to the General," a voice said outside the driver's side window.

"Special circumstance," Will replied.

She felt the ring lift from her neck and drop back down.

"Clint will want to talk to her," the voice said, surprised.

"That was my thought," Will replied, putting the SUV back into drive.

"Who's Clint?" Emily asked as the SUV began to move once more.

"Our president," Will answered.

"President?" Emily asked, surprised.

"We do have some orders for us," Will laughed. "Otherwise, this mob would be complete chaos."

"And you are?" Emily asked calmly.

"Vice president," Will replied. "Billy, that brute back there is just a grunt."

"What about Shawn?" Emily asked.

"Master at Arms," Will said, sounding like he was smiling. "He didn't tell you?"

"He wore the vest," Emily explained. "But thought you were all gone and said it was part of his past. He didn't talk about it much."

"He never was much of a talker," Will laughed. "But the best at strategy I've ever seen."

Suddenly, the SUV stopped, and she heard the engine turn off. The SUV door opened and shut just moments after. She sat silently with the others for several minutes before the doors opened again. The bandana was removed from her eyes, and she squinted in the bright sunlight.

"Let's go," Will said, taking her arm and helping her out of the SUV.

"What about my friends?" Emily said, turning back to see them all still blindfolded.

"Clint just wants you right now," Will said firmly, moving to close the SUV door.

Marley pushed his way out of the door before it closed.

"I don't go anywhere alone," Emily said firmly.

"Just don't let him bite anyone," Will said, slamming the door. "That ring won't save you from that punishment."

She nodded and patted her leg to call Marley to her. Marley walked over and stood firmly beside her. She followed Will into a bar, or what had been a bar before the flash.

The inside was relatively dark, and the tables were filled with men, all wearing the same leather vest. Will led her and Marley through the maze of tables to the front.

"Is this her?" A man Emily assumed was Clint asked.

"Yeah," Will said, turning a chair around and sitting in it backward.

"Never thought I'd see Shawn have an old lady, even before the world went to shit," Clint said, looking her up and down.

"What is that?" Emily asked, frustrated.

"What?" Clint laughed. "Old lady?"

"Yes," Emily replied.

"It means you belong to Shawn," Cole explained. "And if any other man touches you, we will ensure he gets the right to end that man." "That's why Billy wouldn't hit me back," Emily said more to herself than them.

"She hit Billy?" Clint laughed.

"Slapped the taste right out of his mouth for calling her a bitch," Will smiled.

"Now that is something I'm sad I missed," Clint smiled. "Nothing compared to what Shawn will do to him for it, though."

Will nodded in agreement as he rested his hand on the table.

"Where is Shawn?" Clint asked, looking back at her.

"The General took him captive yesterday," Emily said, confused. "That's what we were doing at the compound. We were going to get him back when your goons brought us here."

"I think Billy may get his revenge on her yet," Clint said, looking back at Will.

"You said no one could touch me or…." Emily began in a panic.

"Unless you pulled that off one of the dead," Clint said, glaring back at her. "Because I know that the General does not have Shawn."

"For a fact," Emily laughed. "I was with him when they came."

"Or you were just a scared girl who found a ring and hoped it would make us protect you," Clint said.

"How can you be so sure that I'm lying?!" Emily asked, frustrated.

"I know the General," Clint said, glaring at her. "We keep his perimeter clean and do some of his dirty work. He provides us with ammo."

"So, he would never take one of your guys?" Emily sighed.

"That's the deal and has been working great since the light in the sky," Clint nodded.

"Except he doesn't see it as taking one of your guys," Emily said, angrily. "He sees it as taking back something you stole from him."

"What do you mean?" Will asked, suddenly looking interested in the conversation once more.

"The General tried to recruit him for a year before joining the club," Emily continued. "Once he joined, he knew there was no way to get to him."

She watched as Clint and Will looked at each other. She could tell that Shawn had told them about the General before and knew that she could have only learned this story from Shawn.

"We ended up with the General's daughter inside our town," Emily continued. "When she learned who Shawn was, they used Dillon to manipulate him."

"Dillon?" Will replied. "We thought he was with Shawn when everything went to shit."

"He lost him in the craziness," Emily continued. "He feels horrible for it and is willing to risk his own life to save that boy."

"It is quite a story," Clint said calmly. "And could be true or a story you stole from someone else."

She pulled her backpack off and set it on the table.

"This is one of the General's phones," Emily said, slamming it on the table. "He used it to blackmail Shawn, and Shawn gave it to me just before he left. These are pictures of Shawn and his grandfather, I took from the cabin we were hiding in for two weeks."

Clint and Will looked at the pictures, while her attention was drawn to something she didn't know was in the bag. She reached in and slowly pulled out Hope's storybook.

"You going to read us a story?" Clint said, turning his attention back to her.

"No," Emily said, setting the book on the table and flipping through the pages.

"This is our first group picture together," Emily said, stopping on a page and pointing to Shawn. "This is Shawn with Hope and me when she was born. Shawn and Hope, when he gave her a vest for Christmas. This is Halloween, and this is Hope's birthday."

"Shawn has a daughter?" Will said, turning the book to him.

"Biologically no," Emily admitted, not wanting to lie to them. "But from birth, he has been the only father she has ever known."

"What was your plan?" Clint asked, looking back at her. "Your little army of four plus a dog against an actual army?"

"I never said it was just the four of us," Emily smiled. "And do you think I have been with Shawn this long and not learned a thing or two about strategy?"

"Where are the rest of you?" Will asked.

"Still out there," Emily replied.

"Probably a bluff," Clint said, looking at the pictures.

"There were six vehicles and a bike," Will replied. "There had to be more than just the four of them."

"Who drove the bike?" Clint asked.

"I did," Emily replied. "They made Shawn leave it behind when they took him. He told me to drive it home. I wanted to give it back to him."

"Where's the girl, Hope?" Will asked.

"Safe," Emily replied.

"Where?" Clint repeated.

"If Shawn wants you to know, he can tell you when he's safe," Emily said firmly.

"In a place where you make picture books," Clint laughed. "Get the others and bring them here."

A few people behind her stood and began to move towards the door.

"I've wanted a reason to kill that old bastard as long as I can remember," Clint said, looking back at her.

"Emily!" Alec's voice rang out from the doorway.

"I'm fine!" Emily called back to him. "I think they are going to help us save Shawn."

"Can we trust them?" Sam asked as he walked up beside her.

"Shawn did," Emily replied.

"Do they know a way in?" Cole said as he mean-mugged everyone in the bar.

"We can get in," Clint nodded. "I just want this little lady to understand the consequences if we find out she's lying to us."

"You still don't believe me!" Emily gasped.

"Enough to get you and fight if Shawn is there," Clint nodded. "If he's not, I will greatly enjoy watching the General torture each of you."

"And when he's safe," Emily said, leaning on the table and looking Clint in the eye. "I will accept your apology."

Chapter 14

Clint and the others quickly set to work getting ready. Emily stood with Marley and the others, watching them. They barely spoke to each other, but somehow everyone seemed to know what to do. Guns were loaded, and the bikes were lined up towards the entrance.

"The night shift is the weakest," Will said, walking toward her. "Half the guys sleep while on duty or just don't show up."

"So, we wait until night to get in," Emily replied.

"We will head out at sunset and get there at dark," Will nodded. "You'll want to reach out to your other people and tell them to meet us by your vehicles."

She reached out and took her walkie from Will. She hadn't even had time to realize that they had taken it. Will said nothing else and walked back into the organized chaos.

"I hope it reaches them," Emily said to the others as she pressed the button. "Can you hear me?"

"Thank God!" Charlie's voice rang back. "Where are you?"

"Safe," Emily replied with a smile. "We had a slight change in plans."

"We can't find three others," Charlie replied.

She knew they had agreed not to say anything specific over the radio in case someone else was listening.

"They're with me," Emily replied. "All safe."

"Where are you?" Charlie asked.

"Not far," Emily said. "Meet us back where we left the cars. We won't be alone."

"More friends?" Charlie asked.

"Maybe," Emily said, looking around. While she wanted to trust these guys, part of her still couldn't put her complete faith in them.

"When?" Charlie asked quickly.

"Dawn," Emily said. Part of not being specific was saying the opposite if you had to be.

"Be safe," Charlie replied in his worried dad tone.

"You too," Emily said as she returned the walkie to her waist.

"I said dark," Will smiled, walking up beside her.

"He knows," Emily assured him.

"No details and the opposite if you have to," Will continued to smile. "Shawn taught you well."

She reached up and felt the ring around her neck. It was all she had of Shawn right now, and it brought her comfort as she wrapped her fingers around it.

"So, we might be friends?" Will asked her, forcing her to pay attention to him once more.

"Yeah," Emily nodded.

"Smart choice," Will nodded. "I know Clint can be a bit...."

"Harsh," Emily offered.

"I was going to say a bit of an asshole, but harsh words," Will laughed. "But it hasn't been easy, especially these past few years." "I understand," Emily nodded.

"Yeah," Will said. "Why don't all of you get into the SUV? We'll let you lead so your people don't shoot us."

"I'll drive," Cole offered, stepping in between her and Will.

Will said nothing as he backed away and turned to leave.

"You can't really trust them," Cole said to her as soon as they climbed into the SUV.

"I trust that they will help free Shawn," Emily admitted. "As far as anything else, I don't know."

"I don't know about this," Alec spoke next.

"Shawn left them after the flash for a reason," Sam spoke.

"He went looking for Dillon," Emily explained. "He has said he didn't agree with them all the time; some of them were bad, but not all."

"And how are you supposed to know which are which?" Cole asked, looking around.

"I don't," Emily admitted. "He can tell me when we get him out."

"And what if this is a trick, and they hand us over as soon as we are inside?" Sam asked, worried.

"Then we're in, and we do what we must," Emily explained. "I don't see another way in where we all survive."

"You got a point there," Alec admitted, leaning back into the seat.

"I know it's not the most ideal choice, but it's the best we have," Emily said, looking at each of them.

Cole and Sam softly agreed and then went silent. She had nothing more to say about it. Her brain was already fast at work, coming up with backup plans to the backup plans for once they got inside.

"Here we go," Cole said, starting the SUV.

She looked up to see that Will was motioning for them to go. She straightened up in the seat as they drove. Will led them along the roads and only fell back once the vehicles appeared. She looked but couldn't see anyone through the darkness, but knew that they were there.

"Marley," Emily said as she cracked the door and stepped out.

Marley jumped into the passenger seat and followed her. She walked slowly towards the vehicles as the rumble of motorcycle engines fell silent.

"Dad!" Emily called out into the darkness.

"Is it safe?" Charlie's voice called back.

"They know how to get in," Emily assured him, looking in the direction of his voice.

"Why would they want to help?" Charlie asked, stepping out of the shadows.

"Shawn was one of them before the flash," Emily explained. "It's kind of a brotherhood pact."

"I don't know about this," Charlie said as footsteps came closer behind Emily.

"They're a little rough," Emily admitted. "But I don't think we have a choice."

"Everyone here?" Will asked, walking up beside her.

"Yeah," Emily nodded, looking back at him. "Where's Clint?" Emily asked, looking around.

"He didn't come," Will said casually.

"I thought…" Emily began.

"I'm sure Shawn told you not all of us can be trusted," Will said, looking at her sternly. "Something like that," Emily admitted.

"Clint wasn't in charge before the flash," Will continued. "Our old leader was found with his throat slit just days after we set up that camp."

"Oh," Emily said, trying to hold back her fear.

"The ones that came, I trust," Will said, looking around. "They'll hold to the code and do what needs to be done."

"What code?" Joe asked, stepping forward.

"I can either explain how this works, or we can get moving," Will said quickly. "We don't have time for a lesson and a rescue." "Let's get going," Emily nodded.

"You stay by me," Will said as he began to walk forward.

"Not a chance," Sam said firmly.

"There's no time to debate this," Will said, visibly frustrated. "We either do this my way or not at all."

"It's fine," Emily assured everyone. "I'm fine."

She could see that everyone was unhappy with her decision as she turned and followed Will.

"Is there a reason you want me in the front with you?" Emily asked after they had been walking for several minutes.

"To keep you safe," Will responded quickly. "Plus, having that dog so close makes me feel safer."

She caught a slight smile on his face in the moonlight.

"Alright," Will said, stopping. "The groups are too large for us all to go in at one spot."

"So, we need to split up," Emily confirmed.

"Two of your people with each of my groups," Will replied. "Once inside, we can work our way through the compound and meet in the middle."

She nodded and turned back to the group. She quickly paired them up and set them with each of Will's groups.

"And you want us to leave you alone with him?" Cole said, looking at Will with disgust.

"I'm not alone," Emily assured him, looking at Marley.

"I don't like it," Cole replied, still glaring at Will.

"Cole," Emily begged. "Please just trust me on this."

"For you," Cole said as he turned and headed to join his group.

"So," Will smiled as he began leading the way again. "You never said, but I'm beginning to think you are the leader of this town you're from."

"You could say that," Emily admitted. She felt that Will had been honest with her up to this point and didn't want to lie to him.

"This town," Will continued. "Does it have room for more people?"

"Yes," Emily said slowly. "For people who can accept the rules and live the way we do."

She knew he was wondering if there was enough room for the club to join Sanctuary. Part of her had seen this coming, but she had hoped to avoid it. At least until Shawn could tell her if it was a mistake or not.

"We're here," Will said. He stopped short, making her almost run into him.

She looked past Will and knew they were in the right spot. The wall was considerably shorter than Sanctuary's but looked strong and defensible. Everything about it screamed military base to her from what she had seen in movies. Even men in military uniforms walked the wall with guns over their shoulders.

"How do we get past them?" Emily asked, looking back at Will.

"Shift change is in a few minutes," Will replied. "There's always a five-minute period where no one is on duty."

"Inefficient for a military mastermind," Emily commented.

"He's gotten comfortable," Will explained. "Figures no one would dare attack them here."

"Then he shouldn't have taken Shawn," Emily said coldly.

"A mistake he'll soon realize," Will agreed. "Let's go."

She watched as the men left the wall, which now stood empty. She followed Will to the wall, where he stopped next to it.

"Up and over," Will said, holding his hands for her to step on.

"What about Marley?" Emily asked, looking confused.

"Once you're over, open the gate," Will instructed. "I'll wait here with him."

She felt hesitant but didn't have a better plan. She placed her hands on Will's shoulders, and he pushed her up to climb onto the wall. She crouched down and looked around. Will had been right about there being no one around. A few fires burned in barrels, but there was no sign of people. She made her way down to the gate, removed the piece of wood used to lock it, and slowly pushed it open.

"See," Will smiled as he and Marley entered. "Easy."

She nodded in agreement as Will closed the gate and returned the lock.

"Where would they keep him?" Emily asked, looking out into the compound.

"The General would keep him close," Will said, walking beside her. "His personal quarters are towards the center."

"Of course, they are," Emily sighed.

"Come on," Will replied as he began his way down the makeshift street.

Military tents lined them on either side. Will stopped by each one and glanced inside.

"There's no one," Will said after several tents.

"That's a good thing," Emily replied, confused.

"Depending on where they are," Will said, looking worried.

"What's going on?" Emily asked.

"I don't know," Will said, looking around. "Just stay close."

She and Marley continued to follow Will down the street, finding more and more empty tents. She could feel Will becoming more and more worried the farther they went. They all stopped when a roar of cheers could be heard a short distance ahead.

"What is that?" Emily asked, looking in the direction of the noise.

"Sounds like a real party," Will replied.

Suddenly, the sound of combat boots on the ground came pounding closer to them.

"Quick," Will said in a rushed voice as he pushed her into one of the empty tents.

Marley followed, and they crouched near the back of the tent. She held her breath as a group of soldiers walked past the front of the tent. Her prayers were answered as none of them stopped to look inside.

"They're not headed for patrol," Will said after being sure they were gone.

"Why would they leave the wall unguarded?" Emily asked, confused.

"Damn good question," Will replied.

"But we have to get moving.

She nodded and followed Will out of the tent, Marley close to her side. The roar of cheers continued, and they slowly grew closer.

"Over there," Will said, pointing between a few tents.

She and Marley made their way to the hiding spot.

"What the hell?" Emily whispered, looking at the source of the cheers.

The area in front of them was brightly lit by several fires. A crowd surrounded an empty patch of dirt, each dressed in a combat uniform. In the center were two men with no shirts, beating the hell out of each other.

"A boxing match?" Emily said, confused.

"No," Will replied, looking at the men. "Just a flat-out fight."

"Why?" Emily asked as she continued to watch.

"I don't know," Will said. "A way to blow off steam or maybe fight for a promotion."

She watched the scene unfolding and couldn't help but think that this was the General's equivalent of her town gatherings. But instead of cookies and good music, the soldiers beat the hell out of each other. The bigger of the two men hit the other man hard, knocking him to the ground. The crowd began to cheer as the winner wiped the blood from his mouth.

"It's over," Emily sighed in relief.

"I don't think so," Will said next to her.

She watched as a large man walked up next to the winner, the loser still lying on the ground, not moving.

"That will get the blood pumping!" the man yelled with a smile to the crowd.

The winner grabbed the loser by the arm and dragged him out of view. She looked at the man and couldn't help but notice that he was the most finely dressed of everyone there.

"The General," Emily said softly.

"That's him," Will confirmed.

"Before our next match, I have an announcement!" the General continued talking to the crowd. "Andrews, front and center!"

She watched as a young man, no older than seventeen, walked from the sidelines toward the General.

"Andrews here joined us with no previous military background!" the General continued. "He came with the simple goal of finding his brother, but has grown to be a valuable part of our army! I am pleased to announce to him that his brother has been found!"

She watched as Andrews's stance softened, and he began to look around.

"Is that Dillon?" Emily asked, glancing at Will.

"Quite a bit taller than I last saw him," Will admitted. "But I think so."

"You found him," Andrews asked the General softly, as if in shock.

"I keep my word!" The General replied loudly enough for everyone to hear. "He is alive but is far from well!"

"What happened to him?" Anderson replied with worry visible even to her so far away.

"He was taken in by a group of nonbelievers!" the General continued. "His mind polluted by their beliefs!"

"I can help him," Andrews pleaded. "Please, just let me see him."

"Of course!" the General smiled. "I have not given up on him, Andrews."

She followed the General's gaze as he looked to the side and motioned to someone she couldn't see. She held her breath and watched as two men dragged Shawn into the circle, feet away from the General and Andrews.

"Oh shit!" Emily said, placing her hands over her mouth.

Shawn was not standing on his own and was only held up by the man on either side of him. His face was swollen and bloody, his clothes ripped and covered in blood. She noticed that he was no longer wearing his leather vest.

"First, we lost him to this cult!" the General said, throwing Shawn's vest onto the ground. "Then, sweet lady temptation drove him to another!"

She couldn't see what was on the photograph the General was holding up, but she knew what it was. Shawn carried a picture of Hope and her whenever he went outside the wall.

"I'll kill you!" Shawn said as he fought his head up to glare at the General. She watched as his expression softened, and Shawn's gaze turned to Anderson.

"Dillon?" Shawn said in shock.

"It's me, brother," Dillon replied, taking a step forward.

"You have to get out of here!" Shawn pleaded with him.

"You're safe now," Dillon replied, trying to calm him.

"Listen to me," Shawn pleaded. "He used you to find me. I won't give them what they want; we will die for it. You have to run."

Dillon looked back at the General, who stood there smiling.

"I hate it when someone steals my best line," the General said, shaking his head.

Suddenly, several military men surrounded Dillon, each hitting him until they had ahold of him, unable to fight.

"What's the code to get in?" the General asked, leaning close to Shawn.

"Fuck off!" Shawn yelled back after spitting blood into the General's face.

The General waved his hand to the others as he wiped the blood away. She couldn't help but wince as the sound of Dillon's arm breaking echoed through the camp. Dillon screamed in pain for only a moment and then glared back at the General.

"He only has so many bones," the General said, looking back at Shawn. "The code?"

"I'm sorry," Shawn said to Dillon.

"So am I," Dillon replied through gritted teeth.

"We're all sorry!" the General laughed. "Now, what's the code?"

"Screw you!" Shawn yelled at the General.

She felt herself lunge forward, planning to somehow stop the men from breaking another of Dillon's bones. Will was quick in grabbing her arm and holding her back.

"They'll kill them!" Emily insisted.

Will said nothing but instead pointed all around. She could see people hiding all around just as they were.

"Just needed to wait for the rest of the cavalry," Will smiled, pulling a knife from his waist.

Chapter 15

"What's the plan?" Emily asked, knowing that Will already had something up his sleeve.

"Your team isn't going to like it," Will said, not taking his eyes off Shawn or Dillon.

"Will it save them?" Emily asked, following his gaze.

"It should do the trick," Will replied.

The sound of another of Dillon's bones being broken echoed around them.

"I'm in," Emily said without hesitation.

"We give the General what he wants," Will said, looking at her. "It will divide his attention enough that we can get all of you out."

"You want me just to walk down there and surrender?" Emily asked, surprised.

"Not surrender," Will smiled. "Just be your normal, charming self."

"Stay," Emily said, looking down at Marley. "Stay with Will."

"He'll actually listen to that?" Will said, looking at Marley.

Marley let out an audible huff of disapproval and moved closer to Will.

"He's unique," Emily said, preparing herself for what she had to do.

"The more you piss him off, the easier this plan will be," Will said as she began to move.

"Shouldn't be a problem," Emily replied as she stepped out of their hiding spot and onto the makeshift road.

She stood tall as she walked straight towards where the General was standing.

"The gate code!" the General screamed at Shawn as she walked closer.

"He doesn't know it, you son of a bitch!" Emily yelled out.

"No," Shawn said, looking at her.

"I knew you weren't dead," the General said as he turned to her with a smile. "But never dreamed you would come here." "Let them go," Emily instructed the General as she looked at Shawn and Dillon.

"Why would I do that?" the General smiled, looking from Shawn and Dillon and back at her. "They brought me exactly what I wanted."

"Let them go, you son of a bitch," Emily said as the anger swelled inside her.

"That's the second time you've insulted my mother," the General said, taking a few steps closer to her. "Do it again, and there will be consequences."

"You think I'm scared of you?" Emily said with a mocking tone.

"You should be," the General smiled. "Or do you think we should all be afraid of you because you walked in here alone?"

"You put your daughter in my town," Emily started, still standing firm. "Put my family in danger, took away my man, and forced me to leave my daughter. You should be scared."

"And why's that?" the General laughed, and the crowd surrounding them joined.

"I have something to fight for," Emily smiled back at him. "And I'm willing to die for it."

"Your town, family, and daughter are already under my control," the General laughed. "Veronica has seen to that."

"I took care of that bitch before coming here," Emily grinned. "You'll have to try harder next time."

"What did you do to her?" the General asked, the smile fading from his face.

"Less than she deserved," Emily replied.

"If you hurt her or my grandson…" the General started.

"Oh, I hurt her," Emily nodded. "But your grandson, your daughter beat the hell out of him on her own."

The General said nothing and blankly stared back at her.

"Let them go, and I'll give her back," Emily said, thinking on her feet.

"And my grandson?" the General asked.

"He stays with us," Emily replied. "I won't let him get hurt by you people anymore."

"You can't do that!" the General yelled.

She felt confident that she had pissed him off and hoped the plan was being implemented.

"Emily," Shawn struggled to call out. "Just run! Leave us!"

"Not going to happen," Emily replied to him. "Do we have a deal or not?"

"No," the General said firmly.

She saw a few of the soldiers begin to move toward her.

"I wouldn't do that," Emily warned them.

"Why?" the General sneered. "Is something bad going to happen? Do you plan on killing them all single-handedly?"

The crowd began to laugh with the General.

"I don't understand all the rules," Emily explained. "But I understand you never touch a member's, old lady."

Shawn's eyes locked with hers as she finished talking. Just then, one of the men grabbed her by the arm hard. She turned to face him just as Will appeared behind the man and struck him over the head.

"She warned you," Will said to the man as he fell to the ground.

Suddenly, several explosions began to happen in different parts of the compound. The soldiers started running in different directions to put out the fires.

"Let's go," Will motioned to her as he turned and began to head towards the General.

"Soldiers!" the General called out.

After glancing around, he realized that his army was scattered and no one would be coming to his aid. He turned and ran into the compound.

"It won't take him long to regain control," Will said as they neared Shawn and Dillon.

As they walked, Will scooped up the picture and Shawn's vest. The men holding Shawn and Dillon suddenly realized they were alone. After a glance at each other, they released them and ran.

"Shawn!" Emily yelled as she ran towards where he lay on the ground.

"How did you…." Shawn said, looking at her.

"I'll explain later," Emily insisted. "We have to go."

She pulled Shawn's arm over her shoulder and held on to him as best she could around the waist. She could see Will helping Dillon to his feet in a similar fashion.

"Let's go," Will said as he started towards the front gate.

"The others," Emily said as she struggled to help Shawn follow.

"They're already out," Will answered.

She did her best to help Shawn keep moving. Marley stood beside her, his gaze

darting in every direction, ready to protect them.
They reached the front gate and found it
standing open. The others must have left it open
for them on their way out. She followed behind
Will as quickly as she could, but Shawn was too
heavy for her to keep up.

"Where do you think you're going?!" The
General's voice boomed out as he grabbed her
by the hair and pulled her backward. Shawn
tried to hold on to her but was not quick
enough.

"You think you can come here and ruin
everything I've built!" The General spat in her
face as he pulled her close to him.

"Yeah," Emily replied as she pulled her
knife from her waist and slid it into the
General's stomach with a violent thrust.

"You shouldn't have messed with my
family," Emily whispered to the General as she
pulled the knife out, and the General slid to the
ground.

She returned to Shawn and Marley and
pulled Shawn's arm over her shoulders.

"You okay?" Shawn forcibly said as they
made their way out of the gate.

"Better now," Emily forced herself to
smile up at him.

She glanced back as they left and could
see that the General's body still lay on the
ground, surrounded by a pool of blood. She
looked forward and saw Cole sitting in the SUV
just a few feet away. Will opened the back door,

helped Dillon inside, and then helped her get Shawn in. Will set Shawn's vest and the picture on Shawn's lap and squeezed his shoulder. Shawn nodded, put his hand over the vest, and leaned back against the seat.

"You'll need to ride his bike," Will said after closing the door. "I don't think he's up to it."

"I got it," Emily nodded, trying to wipe the blood from her hands onto her blood-soaked shirt.

"I'm supposed to bring you all back to camp," Will said softly.

"They need a doctor," Emily said in a panic.

"And you have one of those back in that town," Will said, looking around.

"We do," Emily confirmed.

"You'd better get going then," Will nodded.

"Are you going to be okay?" Emily asked, thinking about how angry Clint would be that he let them go.

"I've survived this long," Will laughed.

"Here," Emily said, pulling the walkie from her waist and handing it to Will. "A few hours east of here, signs lead to Sanctuary. When you get close, just radio in, and they'll guide you there."

"This is dangerous," Will said, looking at the walkie. "Are you sure?"

"Yeah," Emily smiled as she walked towards the motorcycle and turned the key. "Just tell Margaret that you're a friend of mine."

Will nodded and tucked the walkie inside his vest. She put the motorcycle into gear and began backing towards the road with Cole behind her. They met up with the other vehicles and started the drive home. She drove faster than she should have in the dark, but she was desperate to put distance between them and the compound.

She breathed a sigh of relief as she made the turn onto the old logging road. As they approached, she heard the gate come to life and open. She led everyone inside and parked the motorcycle.

"We expected you all back hours ago," Julia said, walking beside her.

"Plan changed," Emily replied. "But we got them."

"Are they okay?" Doc asked, joining them.

"Dillon has some broken bones, and Shawn could barely stand," Emily said, climbing off the motorcycle and heading towards the SUV. Alec was already helping Shawn on one side, and Cole was helping Dillon on the other. They all moved quickly to get them to the clinic and stepped out to let Doc get to work.

"Maybe Doc should take a look at you, too," Julia said, looking at her clothes.

"It's not mine," Emily assured her.

"What happened out there?" Julia asked, looking around at all of them.

"A lot," Emily sighed. "But we all made it out. That's all that matters."

"Is it over then?" Howard asked, joining them.

"I don't know," Emily admitted. "But they can't get to us in here even if they try."

The crowd around them began to grow, each shouting questions to get more details. She put her hands over her ears, trying to stop the voices from bombarding her all at once.

"Enough!" Charlie yelled out over all of them. "We've all had a long day, and now is not the time."

As she lowered her hands, Charlie walked over and put his arm around her.

"She hasn't had a moment to breathe in weeks," Charlie continued. "Give her a moment to breathe, and she will explain things when ready."

Everyone mainly stayed silent as they began to walk away. A few offered apologies and told her that they were glad she was home. She leaned against the wall of the clinic and slid to the ground. She allowed herself to cry with deep and heavy sobs. Charlie said nothing as he sat down beside her and held her.

"Emily?" Doc's voice came from the doorway.

"Are they alright?" Emily asked, drying her face and standing up.

"Dillon has two breaks in his right arm and some minor cuts and bruises," Doc said as he took off his glasses and cleaned them.

"And Shawn?" Emily asked quickly.

"They worked him over pretty good," Doc sighed. "Several of his ribs are cracked, and he has a lot of bruising and cuts. Thankfully, nothing was broken."

"So, they are going to be okay?" Charlie asked beside her.

"They just need to rest and heal," Doc nodded.

"What about Steven?" Emily asked next. "Any change?"

"He still hasn't woken up," Doc sighed. "We won't know much more until he wakes up." "Is Hope still with him?" Emily asked. "She hasn't left his side," Doc nodded.

"Can I see them?" Emily asked, almost afraid of the answer.

"Of course," Doc nodded. "But try to keep them relaxed.

"I will," Emily nodded.

"I'll wait here," Charlie said, leaning against the clinic.

"Thanks," Emily replied as she walked inside.

"The guys are in room one, and Steven is in room two," Doc said as he followed her inside.

She wanted to see Shawn more than she could bear, but knew she had to go to Hope first. She slowly opened the door to room two and found Hope asleep in a chair next to Steven.

"Hope," Emily whispered as she closed the door.

"Mommy?!" Hope yelled as she shot up from the chair.

"Hey monkey," Emily smiled at her as she kneeled beside her.

"He hasn't woken up yet," Hope said, looking at Steven.

"I know," Emily said, squeezing her hand. "Thank you for taking care of him while I was gone."

"Did you find Daddy?" Hope asked, looking back at Emily.

"I did," Emily smiled at her. "He's a little hurt, but Doc says he'll be fine."

"Can I see him?" Hope asked, scooting forward in the chair.

"Doc says he needs to rest tonight," Emily smiled at her. "But you and I can bring him breakfast in the morning."

"Are you okay?" Hope asked as she reached for her blood-soaked clothes.

"Yeah," Emily assured her.

"Is that daddy's blood?" Hope asked with tears in her eyes.

"Some of it," Emily said, looking at her clothes. "But he's okay now."

"Hope," Emily asked after a few minutes.

"Did you put your storybook in my bag?"

"Yeah," Hope said, looking down. "I wanted you to have it in case you were gone a long time again."

"Thank you," Emily said with all of her heart.

"Did it help?" Hope asked, looking at her mom.

"You saved us," Emily smiled at her.

Hope smiled, and she could tell that she was proud of herself.

"Why don't you stay with Steven a few more minutes while I check on Daddy?" Emily smiled back at her. "Then we will both go home."

"Can we stay somewhere else tonight?" Hope asked. "I'm not ready to go back there yet."

"Sure," Emily nodded. "I'll ask Grandpa if we can stay with him."

Hope nodded in agreement as she sat back in her chair. Emily stood up and made her way towards the door. She worked hard to hide her anger as she walked out. She had always made their house a haven for Hope. Now, Veronica and Chad had managed to ruin even that. She made her way to room one and walked inside.

"Emily?" Shawn's voice sounded rough as he spoke.

"I'm here." Emily walked over and took his hand.

"Are you okay?" Shawn asked, looking at her with concern.

"I'm fine," Emily assured him with tears in her eyes. "I'm just happy you're safe."

"I knew you'd come," Shawn said, looking at her. "I expected you and everyone from Sanctuary."

"Of course, I was coming," Emily smiled at him. "You didn't think I'd just let you go that easy, did you?"

"No," Shawn lightly smiled. "I know you better than that. But I didn't expect...."

Shawn began to cough, and she could see the pain in his face.

"You didn't expect me to show up with a bunch of bikers," Emily finished for him.

"Especially those bikers," Shawn replied as his coughing stopped. "How did you end up with them?"

"They found me," Emily admitted. "They apparently did work for the General. They said they had no idea that you or Dillon was inside."

"You're lucky they didn't kill you," Shawn coughed and winced in pain again.

"One almost did," Emily admitted, thinking back to the big guy. "But Will saw this and knew it was yours."

"You lucky he was there," Shawn sighed.

"It wasn't enough proof for Clint," Emily admitted. "But Hope hid her storybook in my bag, and the pictures inside were enough to get their help."

"Clint?" Shawn said, confused.

"Apparently, he's the new president," Emily explained. "Will said the last one was killed, and Clint took over."

"Shit," Shawn said, leaning hard against his pillow.

"Nothing to worry about now," Emily said, running her hand through his hair.

"Do they know where we are?" Shawn asked, looking back at her.

"Just Will," Emily said. "He let us go when Clint had ordered him to bring us back to the camp. I gave him general directions and my walkie."

"You need to keep everyone inside," Shawn said firmly. "It's not safe."

"Did I do wrong?" Emily asked, looking at Shawn with concern. "Is Will one of the ones I shouldn't trust?"

"No," Shawn assured her. "He's one of the good ones, and I'm glad he was there. It's Clint that I'm worried about."

"So, you two just going to keep talking like I'm not here?" Dillon's voice came from the next bed over.

"Probably," Shawn said without looking at him.

"Well, just as gruff as ever," Dillon quickly responded. "Maybe I want to talk to the pretty lady."

"She's spoken for," Shawn smiled at Emily. "Try anything, and I'll break the other arm."

"So violent," Dillon laughed.

"I should let you get some sleep," Emily smiled. "I'll be back first thing in the morning."

"You can stay," Dillon smirked from his bed.

"I don't know if he'll survive that long," Shawn said, looking back at her.

"Remember, you wanted to find him," Emily teased. "Good night."

She left the room and took Hope outside to Charlie.

"We were wondering if we could stay with you tonight?" Emily asked as Charlie stood up to greet them.

"Of course," Charlie smiled. "I warn you, though, your grandma snores."

Chapter 16

Emily woke the following day to the sound of hushed voices. She sat up slowly from the couch and saw that Marley was still lying on the floor beside her. She reached down and patted him on the head before swinging her feet around to the ground. She looked down at her dried, blood-stained clothes and immediately remembered the previous night's events.

"They've just about got breakfast ready," Charlie said, walking into the room. "Jessica dropped off some clean clothes for you."

"Thanks," Emily said, taking the clothes from her dad.

"You go get cleaned up," Charlie insisted.

She slowly stood from the couch and made her way to the bathroom. She slowly closed the door behind herself and turned towards the mirror. Her hair, normally kept fairly neat, was a matted mess. The dried blood on her clothes and skin made her look like she had just walked off a horror movie set.

She pulled the chain with Shawn's ring from around her neck and set it on the sink. She turned on the shower to warm up while slowly peeling off her clothes. She then stepped under the water, closing the curtain behind herself.

She stood for a long time, watching the water turn a rust color around her feet. Only when the water began to clear did she move to start washing.

She tried to focus on the task and not think about what had happened the night before. She could still feel the knife in her hand as she stabbed the General. She could still see his body lying in the dirt, surrounded by blood. She could still hear Dillon's bones breaking as they tortured him.

"Emily!" Christine's voice came from the door.

"Almost done!" Emily called back her mom.

She shut off the water and quickly got dressed. Her hair took some work to get straightened out, but soon she was back to looking like herself. She could hear Hope laughing as soon as she opened the bathroom door. A sound that she didn't realize just how much she missed. She made her way to the kitchen and sat down at the table.

"We didn't have any dog food," Christine smiled at her.

"He likes what we're eating just fine," Charlie insisted.

"He deserves a treat," Emily smiled at them.

"We're going to go over today and clean up your place," Christine smiled at her. "Some of the girls are going to meet us there and give us a hand."

"I appreciate that," Emily nodded as she forced herself to take a bite of breakfast.

"And I'm going to move all Shawn's stuff back out of the apartment," Charlie added. "It's time he moved back home."

"Thanks," Emily smiled again.

She knew they were all trying to help and get life back to normal. However, she wasn't in the same place as them. She was still out there, pretending to be dead, making deals with a biker gang or in the compound with the General.

"Is everyone still in the cells?" Emily asked after forcing herself to take another bite.

"Yeah," Charlie nodded. "No need to worry about that, though. They can wait until you're ready."

She nodded, and she forced herself to take one more bite.

"I'd better get over to the clinic and check on everyone," she said as she stood up.

"We made their plates," Hope said as she hurried to join her.

She followed Hope to the counter and picked up the two plates.

"I'll stop by the clinic when we're done here," Christine smiled at her. "Hope can help us set up a room for Steven when he's better."

"Is that okay with you?" Emily asked, looking down at Hope.

Hope nodded in agreement with a smile.

"Alright," Emily smiled. "We'll see you in a bit then."

She walked with Hope and Marley out the door and headed towards the clinic.

"You sure you're okay going home?" Emily asked Hope as they walked.

"It won't be easy," Hope said, looking up at her. "But Grandma told me about what you did to your old house when Chad made things hard for you. How you and the family fixed it up and made it a place that you felt safe."

She had nearly forgotten about that weekend renovation all those years ago. It hadn't been her plan at the time, but maybe fixing that place up did play a part in her newfound strength.

"And don't forget Marley," Emily added. "He helped, too."

"Yeah," Hope laughed as Marley licked her face. "Maybe I'll take him with me today."

"It's fine with me," Emily smiled at her.

Hope ran ahead and opened the clinic door for her. She followed Hope all the way to room one, where Hope opened the door once more.

"Good morning," Emily smiled as she walked in.

"Morning," Dillon smiled back at her.

"Good morning," Shawn said, rolling his eyes at Dillon.

"Thought you guys might be hungry," Emily said as she handed each a plate.

"Actual food?" Dillon said, looking at the plate and then back at her.

"No," Emily teased. "But it looks real, doesn't it?"

"I haven't had anything but MREs for years," Dillon said as he took a bite. "Daddy?" Hope said as she walked into the room.

"Hey, monkey!" Shawn smiled, setting his plate aside and holding out his arms.

She watched as Hope ran over to Shawn and crawled into his lap.

"I'm so sorry," Shawn said as he hugged her tight.

"New rule," Hope said, pulling away from him. "No more lying to protect each other." "I thought I was doing the right thing," Shawn said, ashamed.

"We're stronger together," Hope said firmly. "Both of you promise."

"I promise," Emily said, taking a step closer.

"I promise too," Shawn smiled at her.

"Me too," Dillon spoke with a mouth full of food.

Everyone couldn't help but laugh as Dillon continued to eat. She watched as Hope talked to Shawn as if nothing had happened. After some time passed, a light knock on the door stopped the conversation.

"Just here to pick up Hope," Christine smiled as she opened the door. "Are you ready?" "Yeah," Hope smiled as she hugged Shawn and jumped off the bed.

"Charlie is moving your stuff out of the apartment for you," Christine smiled at Shawn.

"He doesn't need to do that," Shawn insisted, straightening up in the bed.

"You can try to stop him if you want," Christine smiled. "But I think he'll win right now."

"Yes, ma'am," Shawn smiled. "Thank you."

"It's our pleasure," Christine said.

Hope waved goodbye as she left with Christine.

"You have a kid?" Dillon asked, setting aside his empty plate.

"Congratulations," Shawn smiled at him. "You're an uncle."

"I just hope she gets her brains from her mom," Dillon smiled at her. "And her looks."

"Oh, my word," Emily laughed as she sat on the bed next to Shawn. "He's obviously feeling better. How about you?"

"I've been worse," Shawn said as he took her hand. "Doc says we can go home later as long as nothing changes."

"Everyone is ready for us," Emily smiled at him.

"Doc told me about Steven," Shawn said, looking at her thoughtfully.

"Hope is setting up the spare room for him," Emily said, looking down. "I hope you don't mind."

"We could use another man around the house," Shawn smiled at her, pulling her face towards him. "I was going to insist on it."

"I'm an uncle again!" Dillon exclaimed from the next bed.

"Shut up," Shawn laughed.

"Forgive me for trying to lighten the mood," Dillon replied sarcastically.

"Uncle Dillon will have to sleep on the couch," Emily couldn't help but laugh.

"Sold!" Dillon said excitedly. "It's got to be better than the ground."

"Maybe the ground would be better," Shawn said, looking at her.

Just then, Doc walked into the room.

"I'm going to need Dillon for a bit," Doc said, looking at them. "I need to put his permanent cast on."

"Take him, Doc," Shawn said quickly.

"I don't know about this," Dillon said, looking concerned.

"If he fights, you just give him something to knock him out," Shawn insisted.

"I don't think that will be necessary," Doc smiled as he helped Dillon into a wheelchair.

"I think I can walk," Dillon insisted.

"And once that arm is in a permanent cast, you can do just that," Doc smiled, pushing him out of the room.

She looked back at Shawn as Doc closed the door.

"How's he doing?" Emily asked now that they were alone. "Really?"

"He's always put on a good act when he's in pain," Shawn explained. "Best just to go along with it and let him talk when he's ready."

"Has he told you anything?" Emily asked, concerned.

"Yeah," Shawn nodded. "He's just not ready to show that side of himself to you."
"I get that," Emily nodded.

"The General really messed with his head," Shawn continued. "It was never him on the phone. The General told him every camp they raided was hiding me, but I escaped during the fight and kept ending up in bad situations."

"The General knew that you two would do anything for each other," Emily replied.

"Yeah," Shawn said softly. "But he didn't count on my old lady showing up with her own army."

"Old lady!" Emily laughed. "I was so confused when they called me that."

"I bet you were," Shawn laughed. "I'm glad Will found you."

"Me too," Emily admitted. "He reminded me a lot of you, especially when we first met."
"He's a good guy," Shawn nodded. "Maybe you could explain to me what exactly happened out there."

She knew he would ask her about it, but hoped to put it off a bit longer. She took a deep breath and slowly began to tell Shawn everything. Shawn did not interrupt her once and let her tell the whole story.

"You can't let them all in here," Shawn said as she finished. "And because of that, none of them will come."

"I know," Emily admitted. "But I had to try."

"And I love you for that," Shawn smiled at her, squeezing her hand. "And I must say, hearing you call yourself my old lady was kind of hot."

"Really," Emily smiled back at him.

"Oh yeah," Shawn grinned. "Come here."

She lay her head down on Shawn's chest.

"We have a lot to deal with," Emily said as she got comfortable.

"Not this second," Shawn replied as he wrapped his arm around her. "Right now, it's just you and me."

She didn't argue. Her mind was here instead of outside the wall for the first time since she returned.

"Alright," Doc said as he walked back in with Dillon. "I think you are all good to go."

"It itches," Dillon complained, pulling at the cast.

"You'd better get used to it," Shawn said as they sat up. "It's going to be on there a while."

"Just make sure they take it easy," Doc said to her.

"I will," Emily assured him.

"Here are some pain pills just in case, but use them sparingly.

"Are we running low?" Emily asked, confused.

"No," Doc assured her. "They're just really addictive."

"Got it," Emily nodded as she took the pill bottle.

She turned back to see Shawn trying to put on his vest with a look of pain on his face.

"I got you, brother," Dillon said, rushing forward and holding the vest for Shawn.

"Thanks," Shawn said, still wincing.

"Are we ready to go?" Emily asked as chipper as she could.

"Yeah," Shawn smiled back. "Let's give the kid the grand tour.

"Kid?" Dillon questioned as they walked out the door. "I'll have you know that I am no longer a kid. I've seen and done things you couldn't dream."

"I know," Shawn replied. "But I don't think you've seen anything like this since before the flash.

Shawn pushed open the clinic door, and Dillon followed them onto the street. Sanctuary was in full swing, and everyone was hard at work. The smell of fresh bread filled the streets.

Some children played while the adults worked hard in the shops.

"What the fuck?" Dillon said, looking around. "This really is a full-on town."

"Yup," Emily smiled. "There's even a farm that produces all our real food."

"With, like, animals and stuff?" Dillon asked, looking around.

"Yes," Emily laughed.

"He said this wasn't possible," Dillon said as he continued to look around.

"He never met Emily," Shawn replied. "She runs this place, keeps it going."

"So, you're the General, hear?" Dillon asked, looking at her.

"Let's not call me that," Emily insisted as the General's face as she stabbed him flashed into her mind.

"Sorry," Dillon said quickly, looking ashamed.

"It's fine," Emily assured him. "You want the grand tour?"

"Please," Dillon nodded as he followed them.

She showed him the different spots, introducing him to everyone as they went. She explained how things worked and tried hard to presume that he would want to stay.

"So, I'll get a job and an apartment," Dillon said as they walked.

"If you want to stay," Emily said, looking at Shawn.

"Why wouldn't I?" Dillon asked, still looking around in amazement.

"You'll stay with us until you're healed," Emily replied. "Then yes, job and apartment."

"Cool," Dillon grinned.

"I have some stuff I need to handle," Emily said, more seriously. "You guys should probably head back to the house and rest."

"What do you have to do?" Shawn asked, confused.

"I have some unfinished business to handle," Emily tried her best to smile. "Nothing to worry about."

"She's a bad liar," Dillon said, looking at her.

"She can't lie to me to save her life," Shawn added.

"The cells are small, and I need to see if I can get any of the people out," Emily explained.

"Who's in the cells?" Dillon asked.

"Ummm," Emily replied, unsure of how to answer.

"The General's daughter, her husband, and some followers she picked up inside the walls," Shawn answered for her.

"They're still alive?!" Dillon asked angrily.

"Some of the people may be innocent," Emily said.

"But Veronica and Chad aren't!" Dillon said, visibly shaking with anger. "It takes two seconds to put a bullet in their brain and be done with it!"

"I…" Emily stuttered. "It's not that easy."

"Bullshit!" Dillon blurted out. "Give me a gun, and I'll do it."

"Hey!" Shawn yelled, stepping between them. "You need to calm down."

"She's handling this with kid gloves!" Dillon yelled at Shawn. "You have to handle these things quickly and without mercy!"

"Is that what the General taught you?!" Shawn yelled back.

Dillon didn't respond, but his locked jaw told her he was even angrier.

"She does things differently!" Shawn continued. "She'll take advice, but you will not tell her how to do things!"

"Is that an order?" Dillon asked through gritted teeth.

"Do I look like the damn General!" Shawn exploded. "It's a fucking warning from one man to another."

She watched as Dillon visibly relaxed slightly.

"Can you handle this?" Shawn asked more calmly.

"Yeah," Dillon nodded.

"You better," Shawn said, turning back to her. "Let's go."

"Are you sure?" Emily asked, looking back at Dillon. "The others can help me handle this."

"I'm head of security," Shawn smiled. "That is if I get my job back."

"Alec hates it anyway," Emily nodded.

"Then let me do my job," Shawn said as he began to walk.

She walked with Shawn and Dillon to the security building. Outside, she could hear Veronica's voice as clear as a bell.

"Their dead!" Veronica yelled. "And if you want to live, you'll let me out before my father gets here!"

"She sounds like she's in a great mood," Emily said as Shawn opened the door.

"Who's there?!" Veronica yelled as she heard the door open and close.

Emily said nothing but walked directly back to the cells.

"Change your mind about saving your little biker boy?" Veronica sneered at her.

"Not exactly," Emily couldn't help but smile as Shawn and Dillon walked up beside her.

"How?" Veronica stammered, taking a step back from the bars.

"How do you think?" Emily asked, stepping closer.

"Emily?" A voice called out from the next cell over. "Emily, I'm sorry."

She turned away from Veronica and moved over to the next cell. She knew this man. His name was Vernon. He had been here for a little over a year now.

"Vernon?" Emily looked at him, confused.

"I had no choice," Vernon insisted. "She said the General knew where my family was."

She knew Vernon's story; he had been separated from his wife and daughter shortly after the flash.

"Let's talk," Emily said as she unlocked the cell.

Chapter 17

She opened the cell door and let Vernon out. The others in the cell with him did not move or say a word as he left. She relocked the cell behind him and looked at each of them. She had not had time to get the names of Veronica's followers before going to the compound. But looking at each of their faces, she knew they had something in common. They were missing people they cared about. Something that the General could use to manipulate them to bring them to his side.

"Let's sit," Emily said, motioning to a chair in the main room. "Have you eaten yet?"

"Yes," Vernon nodded. "Ms. Julia brought us breakfast already."

"Are you thirsty?" Emily asked as he sat down.

"A little," Vernon nodded.

She grabbed a bottle of water from the shelf and handed it to him as she sat down. She waited as Vernon opened it and drank half the bottle.

"This is an interrogation?" Dillon whispered to Shawn, barely loud enough for Emily to hear.

"A conversation," Shawn replied. "It's what makes us different from them."

"What happened, Vernon?" Emily asked once he had placed the lid back on his water bottle.

"It was right after the break-up," Vernon began, looking between her and Shawn. "Veronica brought me a cell phone and said it was for me. I took it, and on the other end was a young woman claiming to be my daughter, my sweet Caroline. Caroline told me her mother had died, but the General saved her."

She could see the tears forming in Vernon's eyes as he spoke.

"We only spoke for a few minutes, and then Veronica took the phone," Vernon continued. "She said that I owed the General for keeping my daughter alive. I would help her with his plan, or he would cut loose the dead weight."

"That's what they do," Emily sighed, looking at the man as he openly sobbed. "They find a person's weakness and use it against them to get them to cooperate."

"Are you sure she's not there?" Vernon asked, looking back at her.

"She's not," Dillon answered, stepping forward. "I know everyone in that compound, and there are very few women, none named Caroline."

Vernon broke down entirely and was visibly shaking as he wept. She couldn't help it as her heart broke for him. He knew that siding with Veronica was wrong. But he was willing to do anything for a chance to save his family. She wasn't any different from him. She had let people risk their lives for a chance to save Shawn.

"It's not your fault," Emily replied as she took his hand. "It just means that she's not there. She could still be out there."

"It's been two years," Vernon said, looking at her with doubt in his eyes.

"And I lost my family the day after the flash," Emily smiled at him. "Anything is possible."

"Is it the same for the others?" Shawn asked Vernon.

"Yes," Vernon nodded. "When I learned they had all received calls too, I knew something was wrong."

"I fell for it," Shawn said, looking at Emily. "It was never Dillon on the other end of the phone."

"Because anyone who lives there wouldn't want their family near them anymore," Dillon replied. "He trains us until we are nothing more than his soldiers. No one wants their family to see them like that."

"What will you do with us?" Vernon asked, looking at her.

"Help you," Emily replied gently. "But we need to trust each other more."

"How?" Vernon asked, surprised by her answer.

"You have to trust that your family is my family, now that you live here," Emily explained. "If you get a clue that they may be somewhere. I will be the first in line to save them."

"I'm no one special here," Vernon replied. "We barely see each other."

"We're still family," Emily answered. "I don't care if you need to knock on my door at one in the morning. I'm always here for you." "Are you saying you will let me stay?" Vernon asked with tears still clinging to his eyes.

"Of course," Emily nodded. "If you promise to trust me, that is."

"I do," Vernon nodded quickly.

"Why don't you head home and take care of yourself?" Emily suggested. "I'll check in on you later."

"Thank you," Vernon replied as he slowly stood up.

She walked Vernon to the door and then headed back to the cells. It was a slow process, but she talked to each person one at a time. She was correct in her assumption. Each of them had a family member they believed was with the General, someone they needed to save. She talked to them like she had Vernon and sent them home.

"That's risky of you," Dillon commented as the last one left. "What if they are lying?"

"We will keep a close eye on each one," Shawn replied. "We give them a chance."

"Still risky," Dillon said, looking uncomfortable.

"Not any more risky than letting you in," Emily pointed out.

Dillon seemed to understand the point of what they were doing now. He nodded in agreement but still looked uncomfortable.

"What is it?" Shawn asked, noticing the same thing she did.

"Do they get a second chance?" Dillon said, looking back at the cells.

"No," Emily replied shortly. "This was their second chance."

"What are you going to do with them?" Dillon asked, looking back at her.

"Nothing today," Emily replied. "Let them stew in there for a while."

"I can handle it if you want," Dillon offered without hesitation.

"Not how it works, kid," Shawn said, putting his hand on Dillon's shoulder. "She doesn't let others carry out a sentence."

"And I don't decide on something like that alone," Emily added. "I talk to the council and get their opinions before deciding."

"Council?" Dillon asked, confused. "I thought you were in charge?"

"I am," Emily nodded. "But a great leader listens to those around them, to those they trust."

"Then the General was a shit leader,"
Dillon replied.

"You can't just leave us here!" Veronica's
voice rang out.

"I can," Emily replied as she walked
towards the door.

"Emily!" Chad called out. "Emily, I'm a
victim too. She forced me to do it to keep our
son safe!"

She felt her blood boil as she quickly
turned and made her way to the cell.

"Keep him safe!" Emily yelled as she
neared the bars. "So, you had no part in beating
the hell out of him?! You didn't help put him in
a coma?!"

"I was trying to teach him," Chad
explained. "She was upset that he wasn't as
smart as Hope. I thought he would learn faster
with a little motivation."

"A little motivation?!" Emily repeated in
disbelief.

"You need to bring him to us," Chad
insisted, looking at Veronica. "He's our son."

"Wrong," Shawn spoke up, stepping
beside her. "He's our son."

"You can't just take him!" Veronica spoke
up, losing her temper. "He belongs to us!"

"You will never see him again," Emily
sneered through the bars.

Shawn put his arm around her waist and
walked towards the door where Dillon was
waiting for them.

"You can't do this!" Veronica screamed from their cell.

Emily didn't even give her the satisfaction of a reply as she walked out the door. She walked with Shawn and Dillon back to the house. Shawn's motorcycle was already back on the porch, and she could hear the voices inside. She opened the door and felt like she was home again.

"Found them!" Rachael yelled, running into the living room.

"Where were they?" Christine asked, taking the stack of pictures from her.

"In the basement," Rachael replied.

"At least she didn't throw them away," Christine smiled as she turned to hang the pictures back on the wall.

Emily stood with Shawn and Dillon in the entryway, watching everyone run around, putting little things back where they belonged.

"You're early," Hope said as she walked out of Emily's office.

"You never gave us a time," Shawn smiled at her.

"It's almost done," Christine assured them.

"It looks great," Emily said, looking around. "Thank you so much."

"It would have taken you weeks to get this place back together," Sarah said as she came down the stairs.

"I think we got Steven's room all ready," Joe said beside her. "He may want to personalize it, but I think it's awesome."

"Of course, you do," Sarah smiled at him. "You're just a big kid."

"What's wrong with that?" Joe smiled back at her.

Emily glanced over at Dillon and couldn't tell if the interactions in the house confused him or made him uncomfortable. He stood silent, his eyes darting around from person to person. She looked at Shawn and drew his attention to Dillon.

"You alright?" Shawn asked Dillon softly.

"They did all this just to make her comfortable?" Dillon asked. "Without orders?"

"To make us all comfortable," Shawn replied. "That's what family does."

"They're all related?" Dillon asked, even more confused, looking around.

"Some by blood," Shawn explained. "Some like you and I are."

"She wasn't just making stuff up with that whole family speech, was she?" Dillon asked, looking at Shawn.

"You may not always like what she has to say," Shawn smiled. "But she is dead honest about her feelings."

Marley came running through the room and straight up to Dillon. Dillon jumped and looked visibly scared. Marley stopped short and froze, his tail still wagging.

"It's alright," Emily assured him. "He may be big, but he's friendly."

"Unless you try to hurt one of the girls," Shawn smiled.

"He said that dogs had all gone feral," Dillon said, still pinning himself against the wall.

Emily didn't have to ask to know that he was referring to the General.

"I don't know about the ones out there," Emily replied. "But I assure you, he's not out for blood."

Shawn reached down and began to pet Marley and play. Marley was excited but kept looking at Dillon to join. After a few minutes, Dillon slowly relaxed and held his hand out to Marley. Marley didn't hesitate and quickly licked his hand several times. Dillon couldn't help but laugh and then petted Marley.

Emily turned her attention back to the house. They had managed to find everything that Veronica had moved or gotten rid of and turned it back into their home.

"We should probably go," Christine said, looking around. "I'm sure you all want to get some rest and settle back in."

"Thanks, Mom," Emily smiled at her.

"It was easier than fixing up the last house," Christine teased as she hugged her.

She said goodbye to each person as they left. She closed the door behind them and felt herself exhale.

"You guys hungry?" Emily said, looking at them all now playing together with Marley.

"Real food?" Dillon asked, looking at her with excitement.

"That's the only kind of food we have, Uncle Dillon," Hope laughed.

"I'll take that as a yes," Emily smiled as she made her way to the kitchen.

She looked through the cabinets and put together a large dinner. Seeing how Dillon had demolished his breakfast, she knew he must be hungry. She set the timer on the oven and quickly made some sandwiches to tide them over. She carried the plate into the living room and saw them all sitting on the floor. Marley was lying between them, exhausted from the playtime.

"Just a little something until dinner is ready," Emily smiled as she held out the plate for each of them to take a sandwich.

Dillon finished it in just a few bites. She thought this might happen and happily held out the plate to offer him the extra one she had made. He took it without hesitation, but ate the second one a little slower.

"Dinner will still be a bit," Emily smiled as they all finished. "You should probably take Dillon to get some clothes."

"Yeah," Shawn nodded as he stood up. "He is starting to smell."

"Hey," Dillon laughed as he stood up as well. "I washed last week."

Shawn grabbed Dillon playfully by the neck and pushed him towards the door. The two of them seemed like brothers as they walked out.

"Is Uncle Dillon okay?" Hope asked after they were gone.

"He will be," Emily assured her. "He's been through a lot."

"Because of the bad man," Hope said, looking at her with concern.

"Yeah," Emily nodded. "But he can't hurt anyone anymore."

"How can you be sure?" Hope asked.

"I made sure he can't," Emily answered, looking away from Hope.

"You had to," Hope said, climbing into her lap. "You can't save everyone."

"Doesn't mean I can't try," Emily smiled at Hope.

"I know, mommy," Hope smiled up at her. "Alright," Emily said, shaking off the sad conversation. "Let's do something else for a bit."

"Like what?" Hope said, looking at her, confused.

"Well, we need to get the spare blankets for Uncle Dillon," Emily said, looking around. "And a pillow," Hope said, jumping up.

"Yes," Emily nodded as she stood up from the floor.

"I'll get the pillow. You get the blanket," Hope grinned as she ran up the stairs with Marley.

Emily moved slowly up the stairs and to her room. She grabbed a spare blanket but didn't head back downstairs. Instead, she turned and sat on the bed. The same bed she had so many fond memories in, but just a few days ago, she had pulled Chad and Veronica from. She could still see the look on their faces when she came into the room, back from the dead.

She pushed the memory from her head, and instantly another one took its place. It was the General's face as she slid the knife into him. She could still feel the warm, sticky blood running off the knife's handle and onto her hand. She still felt how smoothly the knife pulled back out of his belly and saw him slump to the ground.

"Emily?" Shawn said as he walked into the room. "Are you alright?"

"Yeah," Emily quickly responded, looking at him.

"Hope says you've been up here a while," Shawn said, looking at her with concern.

"I must have spaced out," Emily smiled as she stood up. "It's been a long few days."

"You've done nothing but smile today," Shawn said, ushering her to sit back down. "You've got something on your mind."

"I was just thinking about the General," Emily admitted as casually as she could.

"You did what you had to," Shawn assured her. "You had to kill him."

"I know," Emily sighed as her chest tightened, rethinking everything. "I don't regret stabbing him."

"Then what is it?" Shawn asked, confused.

"I had to kill him," Emily replied with tears in her eyes. "But I don't think I did."

"I saw it with my own eyes," Shawn insisted. "There's no way he survived that."

"I don't think he's dead," Emily replied with more fear than she cared for. "And if he's still alive, he'll regroup and be on his way here."

"That's why you aren't ready to deal with Veronica and Chad," Shawn said, understanding. "In case you need them as a bargaining chip."

"Yes," Emily admitted, looking down at herself, wringing her hands. "I know it's dangerous, but isn't it more if I don't wait?"

"I honestly don't know," Shawn replied, taking her hands. "But I stand by your decision."

"Everyone always does," Emily said, frustrated. "But what if I'm wrong?!"

"What if you are?" Shawn asked calmly. "Who's to say that you're not?"

"That isn't helpful," Emily said, pulling her hands back from him.

"What happened to that warrior woman everyone told me reappeared at the gate?" Shawn asked with a slight smile.

"The adrenaline wore off," Emily replied. "And she sees mistakes she made."

"She saved two people," Shawn said, retaking her hands. "Did what she had to with no casualties and got us inside the wall, where no one can hurt us."

"Except me," Emily replied, looking at him through teary eyes.

"Never," Shawn said firmly. "You would rather die than hurt your family."

She nodded in agreement, but she couldn't help how she felt. She knew deep down that she didn't kill the General. He was still alive and would be coming for them.

"And if the old bastard did survive," Shawn said, pulling her gaze back to him. "We will handle it together."

"Yeah," Emily nodded, trying to smile.

"Speaking of together," Shawn said, standing and pulling her to her feet. "You need to get to your mom's and get ready." "Get ready?" Emily replied, confused.

"We promised," Shawn smiled at her. "As soon as we got back, remember?"

"You want to get married?" Emily asked him, surprised.

"Father Nathan is waiting for us, and everyone else will be ready within the hour," Shawn nodded back. "If he did manage to survive, let's not give him the chance to delay this another second."

"I..." Emily began, unsure of what to say.

"You do still want to marry me, right?" Shawn asked, stepping closer.

"Yes," Emily smiled back.

"Then why wait?" Shawn grinned.

"You're right," Emily laughed, wiping away the last of her tears. "See you at the church."

Chapter 18

She went downstairs, where Hope and Marley were waiting for her.

"Let's go," Emily smiled as she ushered them out the door.

"You and Daddy are really getting married?!" Hope asked with excitement as she ran next to her.

"We sure are," Emily smiled down at her. "If we can get ready."

"Faster, Marley!" Hope called back to the dog.

Marley quickly ran ahead of them, only slowed slightly when he saw they were falling behind. Emily ran with them into her parents' house, where everyone was already busy getting ready.

"Your dress is in our room," Christine smiled at her as she rushed her up the stairs. "Hope yours is in the bathroom."

"Yes, Grandma," Hope said as she took off to get ready.

"A bit more notice would have been nice," Christine smiled as she closed the bedroom door behind them.

"We tried that," Emily smiled.

"Something always seems to get in the way."

"Then spontaneous it is," Christine said.

A few minutes later, Rachael joined them, and they began working together to style her hair.

"Are we too late?" Julia asked as she, Sarah, and Jessica came through the door.

"Just finished her hair," Rachael smiled at them.

Emily couldn't help but smile as they quickly helped each other style their hair and put on their dresses.

"Your turn," Julia smiled as they all turned to her.

Emily allowed them to help her with the wedding dress, shoes, and veil.

"It's perfect," Christine smiled at her with tears in her eyes.

Emily turned and looked at herself in the mirror. Margaret had done a fantastic job on the dress. It had a long, thick-flowing bottom that reminded her of a princess dress. The top was covered in beadwork around the neckline. She was thankful that there were no sleeves as hot as it was outside. The dress did show a few of her bite scars, but right now, she didn't mind. She couldn't help the few tears that welled up in her eyes.

"No crying," Rachael insisted as she dabbed her eyes with a tissue.

"We'd better go," Christine gasped as she looked at the clock. "It's nearly time."

Emily turned as a few girls grabbed the big dress and helped her down the stairs. She was proud of herself for not tripping as she reached the living room.

"Wow," Hope gasped as she looked at Emily.

"Wow, yourself," Emily smiled at Hope, dressed in her flower girl dress.

"I think the most impressive is this guy over here," Joe added from across the room.

"What did you do?!" Emily laughed as she looked at him.

Marley was sitting by Joe's feet, wearing a tuxedo top and wagging his tail.

"I think he looks awesome," Joe laughed, petting Marley on the head.

"Everyone looks great," Charlie laughed, joining them. "But maybe we should get to the church."

"Yeah," Emily smiled, gathering back up the front of her dress. "Let's do this."

The girls helped her gather up the rest of her dress so it would not get dirt all over it on the way to the church. They quickly went down the empty streets and onto the church steps. She couldn't help but notice that no one was on the wall.

"Just for the ceremony," Sam assured her as she looked around. "We have a schedule for as soon as it's over."

"Right," Emily nodded, looking back at the church doors.

"Just focus on this," Julia said, squeezing her hand.

"Right," Emily nodded again, still feeling nervous.

"You ready?" Charlie asked with a bit of concern.

"Definitely," Emily smiled.

"I'll let them know," Sam smiled as he walked back into the church.

"See you inside," Christine smiled as she headed in.

Emily waited, clinging to Charlie's arms as the bride's maids went in with the groomsmen. Finally, Hope walked in with Marley by her side.

"I couldn't say this last time," Charlie said once they were alone. "But I couldn't be happier for you."

"Dad," Emily said, looking at him through her veil.

"Shawn's a good man," Charlie smiled at her.

"I know, Daddy," Emily smiled at him. "I'm glad you're here."

"Me too," Charlie continued to smile. "I wouldn't miss this for the world."

She heard the music change on the other side of the doors.

"You ready?" Charlie asked, offering her his arm.

"Yes," Emily said, taking his arm.

They took a few steps toward the door, and she suddenly had a new fear.

"Daddy," Emily said, pausing for a moment.

"What's wrong?" Charlie asked, looking at her.

"Promise you won't let me fall?" Emily said with genuine concern in her voice.

"Never," Charlie assured her as he took another step forward. "And you don't let me fall either."

She couldn't help but laugh as the church doors opened and they walked in. Everyone in Sanctuary had crammed into the church to watch. They all stood on either side, some with tears in their eyes as she walked in. She couldn't focus on any of their faces. Her attention was focused on the front of the church. Where Shawn stood in a nice tux with his leather vest over the top of it. He was all that mattered at this moment, and the isle felt eternally long as she walked up.

Finally, when they reached the end, she felt herself breathe again as Shawn took her hand and walked her up to the altar. She heard Father Nathan begin to speak, but could not focus on the words. She couldn't take her eyes off Shawn or believe they had finally made it here.

"I do," Shawn said, his eyes still locked with hers.

Shawn looked down briefly as he slid his ring onto her finger. She suddenly realized they had reached the vows, and it was her turn. She waited as Father Nathan spoke, eager to agree.

"I do," Emily answered with a smile she was sure would not fade anytime soon as she slid her ring onto Shawn's finger.

She looked back at Shawn as soon as she finished and waited for Father Nathan to reach the end.

"I now pronounce you husband and wife," Father Nathan announced. "You may kiss the bride."

Shawn didn't hesitate as he lifted her veil and pulled her close. She wrapped her arms around his neck as he lifted her and kissed her. She temporarily forgot where they were or that everyone was watching them. All she knew then was that she was finally married to the man she loved.

She had no idea how long they had kissed when they finally pulled apart and smiled at each other. Emily only wished that she could have stayed like that forever.

"We did it," Shawn smiled at her as he looked back into the church.

She followed his lead and saw everyone standing again, clapping, and even more tears. Shawn took her by the hand and began to lead her down the aisle. She quickly glanced over to see Dillon picking up Hope and following them. She knew that Hope was safe and focused back ahead of herself. As soon as they were outside the church, Shawn quickly picked her up and spun her in a circle. She held onto his neck and laughed as they turned.

Everyone began to file out of the church. She was barely aware of them, though. Some went to the wall, and others went to the main street. Shawn set her back down on her feet, but they still had not let go of each other.

"Take your time," Father Nathan smiled at them as he walked out. "It's your day after all."

"We will," Emily said, not looking away from Shawn.

Father Nathan smiled as he headed towards the main street, leaving them alone. She heard the music turn on, but still had no intentions of moving.

"We did it," Shawn repeated as he looked at her. "We finally got married."

"And nothing got in the way," Emily smiled back at him.

"I didn't know I could be this happy," Shawn smiled, tucking a loose hair behind her ear.

"We've got forever now," Emily smiled at him. "No more being pulled apart."

"Never," Shawn said as he pulled her into another kiss.

She hated it when they parted. It was like he was too far away.

"We should probably get to the party," Shawn smiled at her.

"They can wait," Emily grinned as she pulled him back into the kiss.

"Come on," Shawn laughed as he picked her up and carried her towards the main street.

Shawn set her down as they neared the party. He took her hand and walked her into the cheering crowd. She gripped his arm as they walked, and he led her into the center of everyone. Shawn took her by the waist as the music changed to a slow song, and they began to dance.

"But you haven't had anything to drink yet," Emily teased as they danced.

"Today, I don't need it," Shawn smiled as he twirled her around, her dress catching in the breeze and blowing behind her.

Everyone around them fell silent as they danced. No one joined them; instead, all stood around them, watching silently. For once, all of the attention didn't make her uncomfortable. She barely noticed them as she and Shawn danced in the street.

Shawn led her to a table as the song ended and pulled out a chair for her to sit. She had no idea how long she had been on her feet at this point, but they were grateful for the break. Shawn sat beside her just as Julia rushed over with a few drinks. They each slowly sipped, and she took a look around at the crowd. Many of them were back on the street/dance floor, having fun. She couldn't help but laugh as she spotted Hope making Dillon dance, something he had not done in a long time.

"Sorry about you guys not getting a honeymoon," Christine smiled as she walked toward them.

"We just did it backward," Emily smiled back.

"Yeah," Shawn nodded. "A two-week honeymoon, followed by a kidnapping and rescue, and the wedding."

"You make it sound so normal," Charlie laughed, walking up beside Christine.

"For us, it kinda is," Emily laughed, looking at Shawn.

Christine and Charlie congratulated them and headed back out into the party. For the next little bit, she and Shawn sat as everyone came by and did the same.

"Time for our dance," Hope said, running up to Shawn. "If you're not too tired."

"Never," Shawn smiled as he took Hope's hand and walked back out to dance with her.

She sat and watched as Shawn picked up Hope, trying to hide the pain it caused his ribs, and danced with her. Her thoughts suddenly pulled to Steven, still unconscious in the clinic. She quietly stood up and slipped through the crowd to the clinic. She made her way to Steven's room and sat down in the chair beside him.

"You're missing one heck of a party," Emily said as she took the small boy's hand. "But we will have another one once you are better."

Steven looked asleep as he lay still in the hospital bed.

"This is a big day for you, too," Emily continued talking to him. "This is the day our family becomes one, you included."

She wiped a few tears from her eyes as she spoke, not letting go of Steven's hand.

"I just want you to know," Emily continued. "That no one will ever hurt you again, I promise."

"How's our boy doing?" Shawn asked as he walked into the room.

"Same," Emily replied, wiping the tears from her face. "Doc says he could wake up at any time."

"And we will be here for him when he does," Shawn said, placing his hand on her shoulder.

"I just needed to check on him," Emily smiled at Shawn. "Let him know some things."

"Don't even try to apologize," Shawn interrupted her. "You never need to apologize for checking on one of our kids."

"Do you think he'll understand?" Emily said, looking back at Steven. "That he's part of our family now, and he's safe."

"It may take some time," Shawn said softly. "But we will prove it to him every day."

"Yeah," Emily nodded in agreement as she stood up. "We should let him rest."

"If that's what you want," Shawn smiled.

"The kids are probably dying to get a piece of cake," Emily laughed as she walked towards the door.

"If you count Dillon as a kid, yes," Shawn laughed.

She walked out of the clinic with Shawn and back towards the party.

"Dinner!" Emily suddenly exclaimed as she remembered putting it into the oven earlier.

"I already took it out," Shawn laughed. "It's in the fridge."

"Thank god," Emily laughed. "The last thing we need is me burning down the house."

"I took it out before I came upstairs to get you," Shawn continued to laugh. "So, stop worrying."

"I'll try," Emily replied.

"Try?" Shawn said, looking at her with one eyebrow raised.

"Yeah," Emily said, putting her hands on her hips. "Try."

Shawn moved fast, but she saw it coming. He tried to scoop her up, but she managed to get out of his reach just in time. She laughed as she ran back to the party, dodging in and out of the crowd as Shawn chased her. Somewhere, she wasn't sure where she kicked off her heels and began to run barefoot. The dress still slowed her down, and eventually, Shawn caught up.

"Where are you going?" Shawn laughed as he wrapped his arms around her waist.

"Nowhere," Emily smiled back at him. "Absolutely nowhere."

Shawn smiled as he spun her around and kissed her once more. She had missed kissing him over these past few months, and her world felt complete.

They spent the rest of the evening laughing and enjoying their newly found bliss. The cake cutting was a blast, and each had a face full of cake. Margaret took all the kids back to her house as they began to wind down, allowing the adults to keep going through the night. It was well after midnight before her body started to show signs that she was way past ready for bed.

"You ready to go home?" Shawn asked as a yawn escaped her mouth.

"I think so," Emily smiled back at him. "Where's Dillon?"

"He's staying with Joe tonight," Shawn grinned at her. "Something about not wanting to be in a house with a newly married couple tonight."

"Oh," Emily replied, realizing the intent behind Shawn's grin.

While they had slept next to each other at the cabin, they had not been intimate since before the breakup. She couldn't help but be a little nervous at the idea of it. Though she didn't know why. She loved Shawn, of that she was sure.

"Let's go," Shawn said softly as he helped her to her feet.

She took his hand and walked up the walkway to the house. She waited as Shawn opened the door and turned back to her.

"Might as well do it right," Shawn smiled as he lifted her and carried her over the threshold.

She giggled as they walked, and he sat her down on the other side.

"Alone at last," Shawn smiled as he closed the door.

She didn't reply as she watched Shawn walk closer to her. She felt butterflies in her stomach as he wrapped his arms around her waist and pulled her close.

"I'm never letting go of you again," Shawn said, putting his forehead against hers.

"You better not," Emily replied, closing her eyes and enjoying the moment.

"Come on," Shawn said as he took her hand and led her towards the stairs.

She followed him, the butterflies subsiding a little. She was nearly halfway up the stairs when her worst fear came true. Her foot got tangled up in the dress, and she fell. She and Shawn laughed as they landed together on the staircase.

"It's beautiful," Shawn laughed. "But we must get you out of it for safety reasons."

"Good luck," Emily laughed. "Do you know how many women it took to get me in this thing?"

"Challenge accepted," Shawn laughed as he stood up and picked her up from the stairs.

Shawn carried her up the rest of the staircase, afraid she would fall again if she tried to walk. He didn't set her on her feet again until they were in the bedroom.

"Let's take a look at this," Shawn said, pulling her hair over her shoulder and walking behind her.

She stood still, silently smiling as Shawn began to unhook and untie the variety of things that held the dress in place. After several minutes, she finally felt the dress fall loose around her.

"They make a husband work for it, don't they?" Shawn said, walking back around to face her.

She looked deep into his eyes and suddenly felt all of the butterflies disappear. She was no longer nervous but completely ready. She released her grip on the front of the dress and allowed it to fall to the floor. She held her hand to Shawn, who helped her step the rest of the way out of it. She walked over to the bed and sat down. Shawn didn't break eye contact with her as he removed his vest and set it on the dresser. She scooted back as he walked towards her and lay on the bed. Shawn climbed up beside her and brushed the hair out of her face.

"I love you," Shawn said softly, looking into her eyes.

"I love you too," Emily replied, pushing her body against his.

Shawn leaned down and gently placed his lips against hers. This kiss was different than any other kiss they had that day. She fell deep into it as Shawn's strong arms wrapped around her. Shawn pulled back for just a moment, removing his shirt as he continued to look at her with soft eyes.

"Forever," Shawn said as he leaned back down and scooped her in a passionate kiss.

Chapter 19

She woke the following day feeling happier than she had in months. Her head rested on Shawn's bare chest, and she could tell he was asleep. She dared not move for fear of waking him. Instead, she looked at their hands, each sporting a wedding band. This morning, life was perfect.

"Good morning, wife," Shawn said softly as he ran a hand over her hair.

"Good morning, husband," Emily smiled as she turned her face to look at him.

"Did you sleep okay?" Shawn asked, looking down at her.

"Perfect," Emily replied, still smiling.

"Me too," Shawn said.

"Do we have to get up?" Emily said as he began to shift.

"I'll be right back," Shawn laughed.

She groaned as she slid off his chest, and he stood up. She propped herself up with her hand and watched him as he walked to the bathroom. Shawn looked back at her, laughing as he closed the door. She lay back on the bed and couldn't help but continue to smile.

"Can we just stay like this all day?"

Emily asked as she heard the bathroom door open.

"If that's what you want," Shawn said, climbing back into bed with her.

"What about Hope?" Emily asked, remembering they had responsibilities.

"Won't be home until tomorrow," Shawn smiled at her.

"You put some thought into this," Emily said, surprised at him.

"Maybe," Shawn smiled as he kissed her lightly.

"So, the plan is to stay in bed, alone, all day and get lost in each other," Emily replied.

"Is that okay with you?" Shawn asked with a grin.

She said nothing as she moved under the sheet and pulled herself up on Shawn. She bent down and kissed Shawn deeply.

"I'll take that as a yes," Shawn said as he pulled her closer.

They again allowed their passion to overtake them and got lost in each other.

"You really are perfect," Shawn said, rubbing her arm as they rested in bed together.

"Not really," Emily replied. "Though, you do make me feel like I could be."

"You know what I feel?" Shawn asked, rolling over to face her.

"What?" Emily laughed.

"Hungry," Shawn replied with a smile. "We won't be able to keep going like this if we don't eat."

With that, Shawn pulled back the sheet and began to pull his pants on. She laughed as she did the same and pulled on a nightgown.

"Just a short break," Shawn promised as he kissed her and walked out the door.

She followed him out of the bedroom and down the stairs. She glanced at the clock as they walked through the living room to see that it was nearly noon. She had barely eaten anything the night before and hadn't realized how hungry she was.

"What do you want to eat?" Emily said, leaning against the counter as Shawn opened the refrigerator.

"Better not let it go to waste," Shawn smiled as he set the dinner she had prepared the night before on the counter.

She nodded in agreement as she grabbed a couple of plates from the cabinet. Shawn put some of the food on each of the plates and slid them into the microwave. She sat down and watched as he poured each of them a drink and set it on the counter.

"You're the one who's perfect," Emily smiled, not taking her eyes off him.

"I know," Shawn smiled, winking at her.

The microwave began to beep, signaling that it was done. Shawn removed the plate and set it in front of her. He then made his own and placed it in the microwave.

"Don't wait on me," Shawn said as he looked back at her. "I eat much faster than you do."

She didn't argue as she picked up her fork and began to eat. Her stomach had been growling since they walked into the kitchen. A few minutes later, the microwave dinged again, and Shawn sat beside her with his plate.

"I was thinking," Emily said as they both finished.

"No," Shawn interrupted her. "No thinking today."

"Really?" Emily said, looking at him, surprised.

"Yup," Shawn replied as he picked up their plates and set them in the sink.

"And how do you plan on stopping me?" Emily asked, staring at him.

"I hoped you would ask that," Shawn grinned as he quickly closed the space between them.

Shawn lifted her out of her chair and sat her on the counter. She knew where this was going, but she still enjoyed the game.

"Was that supposed to scare me?" Emily teased.

"No," Shawn said as he pushed her hair over her shoulder.

"Then what's your plan?" Emily continued to tease. "Because I'm still full of thoughts."

"Not for long," Shawn grinned as he pulled her closer.

"Still thinking," Emily mocked as she wrapped her arms around his neck.

Shawn grinned a devilish smile and leaned in to kiss her.

"Shawn!" Dillon's voice rang out before their lips could touch.

"Son of a bitch!" Shawn cursed as he slowly pulled away from Emily.

"Shawn!" Dillon's voice rang out once more, closer this time.

"Don't you dare move," Shawn warned her as he turned and headed out of the kitchen.

"You can't tell me what to do," Emily shot back, causing him to glance back at her with that devilish smile once more.

She leaned back on her hands while sitting on the counter. She could hear Shawn and Dillon talking in the next room, but didn't pay close enough attention to know what they were saying.

"I'm sorry," Shawn said, walking back into the room, looking frustrated.

"What's going on?" Emily asked, sliding off the counter.

"We need to get dressed and get to the wall," Shawn replied, genuinely remorseful.

"Is something wrong?" Emily asked as Shawn turned to leave the kitchen once more.

"Maybe," Shawn replied, waiting for her to catch up. "Clint is at the gate with the club."

"All of them?!" Emily asked as she followed him up to the bedroom.

"Most," Shawn replied as he quickly pulled on a shirt and began putting on his boots.

She had many more questions, but knew they would all be answered soon. She quickly dressed and ran to the bathroom to put up her hair. When she returned to the bedroom, Shawn was waiting for her, ready to go.

"I'm sorry," Shawn repeated as soon as he saw her.

"Stop," Emily insisted. "They're here because I gave them directions and asked for their help."

"To save me," Shawn said, looking ashamed and frustrated simultaneously.

"I would have asked the devil himself if that's what it took," Emily insisted, getting frustrated. "Now, let's handle this and get back to what we were doing."

"Together?" Shawn smiled at her softly.

"Forever," Emily smiled back, taking his hand.

She and Shawn made their way downstairs and outside.

"I'm sorry," Dillon said as soon as they walked out. "I hope I didn't interrupt anything."

"You did," Shawn answered. "Let's get this done so we can get back to it."

"Shawn!" Emily gasped, surprised at how blunt he was being.

"I'm used to it," Dillon replied, following them down the stairs.

"Really?!" Emily said, looking at both of them.

"Not like that!" Dillon replied, panicking.

"Uh-huh," Emily said, looking at Shawn, who was glaring at Dillon.

"I have no idea what he is talking about," Shawn said, trying to defend himself. "Kid must have hit his head out there."

"No, I didn't," Dillon said, not thinking.

"Keep talking, and you will," Shawn said in a warning tone.

"Brothers," Emily said, rolling her eyes as she headed up the stairs on the wall.

She could still hear them talking as she reached the top and could see that everyone had been called to the wall.

"He's demanding to talk to you," Sam said, walking closer.

"Demanding?" Emily replied, looking down. "Do they have the walkie?" "No," Sam said, shaking his head.
"Apparently, Will and half the club are missing. He thinks you have them in here."

"Missing," Emily repeated to herself.

"More like left," Shawn said, walking up beside her. "Probably on their way here."

"What do we do?" Emily asked, looking at him.

"Let me go out and talk to them," Shawn said, rubbing her arm and then turning back towards the stairs.

"I'll go with you," Emily said, jogging to catch up with him.

"No," Shawn said as softly as he could. "It's not safe."

"We do things together," Emily insisted. "And how safer could we be with Margaret watching our backs?"

Shawn looked over her shoulder to where Margaret sat with her rifle pointed.

"Alright," Shawn finally conceded before heading down the stairs.

She followed behind him, almost having to run to keep up. She walked with Shawn to the outer gate just as it opened enough for the two of them to walk out.

"Good girl," Emily smiled, looking up towards where Hope would be in the control room.

There were several people, including Cole, standing in the in-between. She knew they were ready just in case Clint and his men tried to force their way in. She turned her attention back forward as Shawn began to walk out.

"Well, bless my soul!" Clint smiled as they walked into view. "You are alive!"

"Clint," Shawn nodded in a stern voice.

"That's all I get?!" Clint sounded like he was faking being insulted. "After everything I've done for you!"

"I didn't see you at the compound," Shawn replied flatly.

She stood silent, watching them. She had never seen Shawn like this. His words were cold, and he stood rigid, looking at Clint.

"Couldn't risk things falling apart if some of us died," Clint smiled.

"Of course," Shawn replied in the same tone. "What do you want?"

"Wanted to make sure you were alright," Clint smiled. "None of our guys came back after the compound."

"We parted ways outside the gate," Shawn said.

She wanted to speak, but felt it wasn't the time for that. Shawn knew this man better than her, and for now, it was best to let him handle it.

"Really?" Clint said, looking like he had just sucked on a lemon. "They were supposed to bring you back to camp, dead or alive."

"Plans changed," Shawn said with no emotion.

"So, you won't mind if we come in and take a look," Clint said, looking at the gate.

She could tell he wasn't asking but demanding.

"I don't think so," Shawn said, standing his ground.

"I thought we were brothers," Clint said, leaning forward on his motorcycle. "We share everything."

She felt dirty with the way Clint was looking at her. Shawn stepped in front of her, blocking her from Clint's view.

"That wasn't the vow I took," Shawn replied once she was safe from Clint's gaze.

"Wow!" Clint said, surprised. "Whatever she's got between her legs has put you on a leash, hasn't it?" Clint sneered, growing frustrated.

"Leave," Shawn replied, still showing no emotion. "Your men aren't here, and you're not getting in."

She remained silent as Shawn turned and began to lead her back inside the wall. Everything seemed quiet until a shot echoed around them. Shawn wrapped himself around her and pushed her back through the gate. She turned to look back as the gate began to close behind them. Clint was looking up at the wall with a terrified yet angry look.

"That was a warning!" Margaret's voice rang down from the top of the wall.

She could see a handgun in the dirt next to Clint's bike just as the gate closed.

"Will and the others never went back," Emily said, looking at Shawn, still shaking.

"Are you alright?" Shawn said, looking at her for injuries.

"I'm fine," Emily insisted. "Are you?"

"Fine," Shawn replied, breathing a sigh of relief.

"If they didn't go back, they should have come straight here," Emily said, talking about Will and the others again.

"No," Shawn said, shaking his head. "He knew that Clint would follow and didn't want us to have to lie for him."

"So, the ones you said weren't safe to let in," Emily began. "They are the ones at the gate, aren't they?"

"Yeah," Shawn said, nodding and looking at the closed gate.

"Letting them in to see the others who aren't here wouldn't do any good, would it?" Emily asked.

"No," Shawn said, shaking his head. "They're not here to find the others; they're here to take over."

"How?" Emily asked, confused. "He had to know that you would tell them no. What's the plan?"

"I don't know," Shawn admitted, looking angry. "But they have to have one."

"Then let's make one of our own," Emily replied.

"Will," Shawn said, realizing what she was hinting at. "If he's out there, we have forces outside and inside the wall."

"Maybe," Shawn said, grabbing his walkie. "Will. Will you be out there?"

"Good to hear your voice, brother," Will's voice returned.

"Yours too," Shawn said, nearly smiling. "We got a bit of a situation here."

"Clint," Will responded quickly.

"Says you guys never returned and thinks you're hiding here," Shawn explained.

"No, he doesn't," Will replied.

"What?" Shawn asked, confused.

"He sent us out," Will explained. "In the opposite direction."

"What the hell?!" Shawn said, frustrated.

"Apparently, he didn't trust us enough to know," Will replied.

"Something's not right," Emily said, looking at Shawn. "This feels like a distraction."

"You're right," Shawn said, looking at the gate again. "You said they were doing work for the General."

"That's what they said," Emily replied. "They knew much about the compound, so it seems legit."

"You still there, brother?" Will's voice came out of the walkie.

Shawn looked at her for a moment. She could tell by the look on his face that he could see the fear in her eyes.

"The General," Shawn said, taking a breath. "Are you able to confirm dead or alive?"

"Negative," Will replied. "Clint went to the compound but sent us out without confirmation either way."

She felt like the wind had been knocked out of her. When she saw him lying in the dirt, she knew that bastard would somehow survive. She looked at Shawn and could see the anger in his eyes.

"Was Clint made president by vote?" Shawn asked Will.

"No," Will replied. "No vote, no loyalty."

She felt her breath return as confusion washed over her. She didn't understand what they were talking about with votes and loyalty. They just discovered that she was probably right; the General was alive, and they chose to talk about this.

"Is this really the time?" Emily blurted out in frustration.

"Trust me," Shawn replied to her, his expression softening.

"Will," Shawn said into the walkie. "I need you, brother."

"On our way," Will replied. "Radio when we get closer."

Shawn returned the walkie to his waist and walked back into Sanctuary. She followed after him, still confused. She knew that Will and the others were on the way. But she still didn't understand what was going on or the plan.

"We need to keep everyone on the wall until they get here," Shawn said, turning back to her.

"I don't understand," Emily said, looking at him.

"Clint took control by force," Shawn explained. "Meaning that the vows we all took are void."

"So, none of you have any loyalty to the club?" Emily asked.

"No," Shawn replied. "But Will and I were close. He'll come with the others and help us."

"They can't get in," Emily said. "We can wait them out and then let Will and the others in."

"We can't trust that," Shawn said. "Clint knew he couldn't get through the gate. He has another plan. You said it yourself. We need a plan of our own."

"But I don't even know the plan," Emily said, frustrated.

"Right now, we don't have one," Shawn admitted. "But we do have forces inside and outside. If nothing else, they can warn us of what we can't see out there."

"Maybe it would be better if we found a way to unite our forces," Emily said.

"First, we get them here, and then we figure it out," Shawn replied shortly.

"I guess the honeymoon's over," Emily said, realizing they wouldn't get to finish what they started in the kitchen.

"We got forever," Shawn said, pulling her close. "We just have to protect it right now."

"Together," Emily smiled at him as Shawn kissed her.

Chapter 20

Time passed slowly as they waited on the wall, Clint and his group still waiting below them. She sent Hope and the other children to the farm to hide in the cellar. She couldn't think of a safer place for them all to hide, just in case things went sideways. She felt like she was going to explode out of her skin just waiting like this.

"We're okay," Shawn assured her as he walked beside her.

"I want them gone," Emily replied, glaring down at Clint.

"I know," Shawn said softly. "Me too."

"I hate just waiting," Emily said, looking at him. "I need to do something."

"Emily. Shawn," Doc's voice came over the radio on Shawn's waist.

"Go ahead, Doc," Shawn answered after grabbing his walkie.

"He's awake," Doc replied.

"Go check on our son," Shawn said, returning the walkie to his waist.

"Are you sure I should leave?" Emily asked with concern.

"You said you needed to do something,"

Shawn replied. "Go check on him." "Right,"
Emily nodded, feeling nervous.

"It will be fine," Shawn assured her. "He needs you right now."

She walked towards the stairs. She wished Marley were with her, but she had sent him with Hope. She made her way down the stairs and to the clinic. She opened the door to find Doc waiting for her inside.

"How is he?" Emily asked, walking in.

"Scared," Doc answered. "He thinks Veronica and Chad will be coming for him.

"Poor kid," Emily said, looking at his door.

"I told him you were on your way," Doc replied. "He's waiting on you."

She steadied her nerves and walked to Steven's door. She took a deep breath and turned the handle.

"Steven," Emily said as she walked in.

She entered the room to see the small boy lying in bed. His eyes were wide with fear, and he didn't relax seeing her. She closed the door softly and took a few steps toward the bed. Steven crawled backward, trying to keep the space between them.

"It's alright," Emily said softly as she stopped. "I'm not going to hurt you."

Steven remained still, his eyes still wide, without saying a word.

"No one's going to hurt you," Emily assured him, hoping he would relax.

"They will," Steven replied, looking at the door behind her. "They always do."

"Not anymore," Emily replied firmly. "I won't let them."

"Why?" Steven said, relaxing just a little.

"I won't let anyone hurt my family," Emily said without a second thought. "You know that."

"But I'm not your family," Steven said, tensing back up.

"Do you want to be?" Emily asked softly. She realized that while she and Shawn had decided to adopt him, they had never had a chance to ask Steven how he felt about it.

"You want to be my mommy?" Steven asked, confused.

"Yes," Emily nodded. "And Shawn wants to be your daddy. If you want to be our son." "I don't have to go back with them?" Steven said, almost in disbelief. "I don't have to be a good soldier?"

"You just have to be Steven," Emily assured him. "You never have to see them again."

"Where are they?" Steven asked, looking at the door again.

"Locked up," Emily replied.

"I want them to leave," Steven said firmly.

She couldn't help but be surprised at the conviction in his words. Being so young, he seemed to understand what happened and what he needed to happen to be safe. She also couldn't help but notice that he talked much clearer than the average three-year-old. While it was clear he was not as advanced as Hope, he was more advanced than Chad, and Veronica gave him credit for it.

"Soon," Emily replied. "We had other issues that we had to deal with first."

"Is the General here?" Steven asked, looking scared once again.

"No," Emily assured him. "But he might be here soon, though."

She decided it was best not to lie to him. She wanted him to trust her, and starting with lies was not a good idea.

"Can you keep him out?" Steven asked, looking at her.

"That's the plan," Emily assured him, taking a step closer.

This time, Steven did not back away. She walked all the way over to the bed and sat down beside him. Steven scooted closer to her as she sat.

"I want to be part of your family," Steven said, looking at her.

"Then you are," Emily smiled at him, pulling him into her lap.

Steven hugged her tight, and she hugged him back. She sat just holding Steven for several minutes before Doc walked in.

"Everything alright?" Doc asked as he entered the room.

"I think so," Emily replied, looking at Steven.

"Yeah," Steven said. "I got a new family, and they'll protect me."

"Good to hear," Doc said, looking at Emily. "All the tests look good," Doc continued, looking at his clipboard. "You just make sure to tell Emily...."

"Mommy," Steven corrected him.

"Right," Doc nodded. "Make sure to tell Mommy if you start to feel pain anywhere or if things seem blurry."

"Yes, sir," Steven replied with a smile.

"Is it okay to put him with the other kids?" Emily asked.

"I think so," Doc replied. "Just tell the older ones to make sure he rests and eats slowly."

"Will do," Emily nodded.

"I can't stay with you?" Steven said, looking at her, concerned.

"I have to go back to the wall," Emily replied softly. "It's not safe for you there."

"Is Hope with the other kids?" Steven asked.

She knew he would refuse to go if Hope was on the wall.

"She is," Emily assured him.

"Can I see my new daddy first?" Steven asked.

"On it," Doc said, grabbing his walkie.

"Uh, new daddy, your son is asking to see you."

Doc winked at Steven as he spoke.

"On my way," Shawn replied.

They didn't have to wait long before Shawn appeared.

"Hey, buddy," Shawn smiled as he walked in. "How are you feeling?"

"Better," Steven smiled at him.

She knew he wanted to confirm that Shawn had agreed to be his new dad. Steven held his arms to Shawn, and Shawn walked over and picked him up.

"Are you going to go with the other kids?" Shawn asked, holding Steven.

"Yeah," Steven nodded. "But I have to rest and eat slowly."

"I wish I could have that job," Shawn laughed. "I'm sure your sister will be happy to see you."

"I want to see her too," Steven said as he hugged Shawn.

"Do me a favor," Shawn said, hugging Steven. "Look after Hope. You are her big brother, after all."

"But Hope is bigger than me?" Steven said, confused.

"But you're older," Shawn reminded him. "Make sure she doesn't get into too much trouble."

"Yes, sir," Steven smiled at him.

"It's time," Alec's voice came over the radio.

"Time for what?" Steven asked, looking at Shawn and her.

"Time to make the bad people go away," Emily answered him, standing up.

"Doc, can you…" Shawn began as he handed Steven to Doc.

"Of course," Doc replied as he took Steven.

"We'll see you soon, buddy," Shawn said to Steven as he opened the door.

"It won't be long," Emily waved after him as Doc ran out of the clinic.

"You ready for this?" Shawn asked as he looked at her.

"Ready or not, it's time," Emily replied as she walked out the door.

Shawn followed behind her, quickly making their way up the wall. She walked to the edge and saw that the bikers were no longer alone. Their numbers had doubled, and they were no longer waiting around. Now, bikers were few in a sea of military uniforms. She scanned them all, looking for any sign of the General.

"He's not here," Emily said to Shawn.

"Cowards never come to the front lines," Shawn replied.

"Brother," Shawn's walkie came to life.

"I'm here," Shawn said after taking the walkie from his waist.

"One heck of a party you have here," Will's voice answered.

"Party crashers," Shawn replied. "Any sign of the guest of honor?"

"Negative," Will answered. "But snakes hide well in the tall grass."

She could feel Shawn look back at her as she went back to searching the crowd below for any sign of the General.

"What's the plan?" Will's voice rang out once more.

"How far out are they?" Emily asked, not looking at Shawn.

"How far out are you?" Shawn asked Will without question.

"Little over a mile. Why?" Will replied.

"Tell them to back up a mile," Emily said, heading for the stairs. "When they see smoke, come back, and we can get them inside."

"How?" Shawn said, following her down the stairs.

She reached the COM building and looked back to see that she had drawn a crowd.

"We can't clear them all out," Cole said, walking in. "And even if we did, it would be a waste of ammo as there are more out there."

"We haven't burned the pits in months," Emily said as she flicked the switch to turn off the outside speakers. "The dead have to be spilling out of the pits."

"Probably," Cole answered, confused.

We can draw them to the wall with sound," Emily continued. "They don't have the firepower down there to fight off a horde like that."

"They'll scatter, but then how do we get Will and the others in?" Shawn asked, still not understanding.

"We have homemade kerosene," Emily continued, looking at all of them. "We pour it over the wall on either side of the gate and light it."

"The dead in front of the gate will be drawn to it," Alec said, understanding.

"Giving Will and the others just enough of a clearing to get in," Shawn said, finally catching up.

"We'll get the Kerosene," Sam said, nudging Alec.

"I need the rest of you to move some of the speakers up on the wall," Emily said as the two of them headed out the door.

"On it," Cole said, walking out the door with Jacob.

"This could work," Shawn said after thinking for a few minutes.

"Only if you get the others back," Emily reminded him, nodding at the walkie.

Shawn quickly grabbed the walkie and gave Will the instructions. She walked outside to see a speaker heading up the wall stairs.

"It will burn hot and fast," Emily said more to herself than Shawn. It should be out before they can spread it to the trees."

"We can keep the sound going to be sure," Shawn answered her. "We get all our allies inside and let the dead pick them off one by one."

"And if they try to find a way in, our numbers will be greater, and we can fight them off," Emily finished.

She and Shawn made their way up the wall and told everyone the plan. No one questioned it and helped put everything in motion. It didn't take them long to get it all set up. Will radioed that they were in position just as everything was in place.

"You guys need anything?" Emily yelled down to the men on the ground.

"A cold beer would be nice!" Clint yelled back at her.

"Fresh out," Emily yelled back. "How about some music?"

"Music?!" Clint laughed back. "Why the fuck would we want music?!"

His laughter made her smile. She nodded at Shawn, who signaled Sara in the COM building. The speakers roared to life, playing heavy metal music. Not her favorite, but it seemed fitting for the situation. She looked down and could see a mixed reaction in the crowd below. Some were confused, while others' heads banged to the music. She looked past them at the tree line, waiting for their surprise army to appear. It didn't take long for a zombie to finally walk into view. One of the soldiers put it down quickly, but more began to ooze out from the trees.

"Turn it off, damn it!" Clint yelled up the wall.

She pointed to her ear to signal she couldn't hear him as she bobbed along to the music.

"Turn it off!" Clint yelled again.

She ignored him this time as she banged along with the music. She watched as the bikers began driving in different directions to escape the dead. Most of them succeeded, and some did not. The soldiers retreated to the east, all of them. She knew he was to the east if the General was here.

They allowed the music to continue a few minutes after all the soldiers and bikers disappeared before pouring the kerosene over the wall. It didn't take long before the zombies ignited on either side of the gate, drawing the ones from in front. Within a few moments, the roar of motorcycles came towards them. She quickly entered the outer gate code and opened it for them to get in. She shut the gate behind them as soon as possible, but some of the dead still managed to get inside. She ran down the stairs to see that Will and the others had dealt with them quickly. Shawn walked straight to Will and wrapped him in a big hug.

"Was a little afraid it wouldn't open," Will said as he hugged Shawn.

"She keeps her word," Shawn smiled as he released Will.

"That she does," Will smiled back at him. "And she got you to put on a shackle!" Will exclaimed, seeing Shawn's wedding ring.

"More like I got her to put one on," Shawn smiled back at Emily.

"Good thing too," Will said, looking at her. "I might have had to try to steal her away."

"Others have tried and failed," Emily smiled as she walked toward them. "Everyone okay?"

"All in one piece," Will said, looking around.

"We still have to do this right," Emily said, looking at Shawn.

"Of course," Shawn nodded in agreement. "Doc will have to examine you before you come in."

"One of the rules," Will said, looking at Emily.

"I warned ya," Emily smiled back.

"What the hell," Will laughed. "It will be the first doctor some of these guys have seen since they were kids."

As if on cue, Doc walked through the gate. He introduced himself to Will and led him to the small examination room. It took a while for him to examine all of the bikers. It was well after the sun had set, and the kerosene burned off the last of the zombies.

"All clear," Doc reported as he walked out with the last biker.

"Doc said you guys had some cabins set up beyond that wall," Will said, pointing to the quarantine area. "I'm sure there are other rules we need to follow. But if it's okay with you, we can just bunk down there until we have time to review them."

"I don't see a problem with that," Emily said after a moment.

Actually, Will's not being eager to get inside Sanctuary made her feel more confident in her decision to let them in. In a way, it confirmed for her that they were on their side. Will motioned the bikers to follow him as they went into the quarantine area.

"Now we really have an army," Shawn said to her as the door closed behind the last of them.

"And an army of zombies between us and the others," Emily added. "But I have no clue what to do now."

"That's simple," Shawn said as he put his arm around her. "We'll go get our kids and head home."

"But what about…." Emily began to argue.

"We will keep the normal watch on the wall," Shawn interrupted her. "They can't get in."

"And we can't get out," Emily reminded him.

"We won today," Shawn sighed. "Let's be happy with that before we move on to the next battle."

"You're right," Emily smiled. "Let's go get our kids."

She waited for Shawn to give instructions to everyone on the wall. Once he returned, they walked with the other parents to get the kids from the farm. Hope and Steven were beyond happy to see them.

"Are we safe?" Steven asked as Shawn carried him into the house.

"We are tonight," Emily answered him with a smile.

She and Shawn put the kids to bed. Steven was thrilled when he saw the room made just for him. They decided to leave both of the kids' doors open, so Marley could wander back and forth as he wanted. She felt like she hadn't slept in a week by the time they got to their room.

"We still don't know their plan," Emily said as she crawled into bed.

"Whatever it was, a wall of zombies will slow them down," Shawn replied as he lay beside her.

"She sent zombies after us!" Clint said, running into a military-type camp. "That bitch is out of her fucking mind!"

"She has a better mind for strategy than I thought," the General said, adjusting in a chair. A large white bandage was wrapped around his stomach with a light pink stain peeking through it.

"What do we do now?!" Clint asked, fuming.

"First, you will stop demanding answers from me!" the General snapped.

Clint took a step back and went quiet like a whipped dog.

"It changes nothing," the General finished.

"We can't get near the gate," Clint explained. "We sat all day and got to see nothing but that wall and the stupid sign. My men died for nothing!"

"Stupid sign?" the General asked, looking at him. "What stupid sign?"

"It had some cute phrase on it," Clint said, frustrated.

"What was the phrase?" the General demanded.

"Why does it matter?" Clint asked, growing angry. "The code wasn't written on it."

"Details are important," the General spat at him. "Miss one, and everything falls apart." Clint didn't understand but thought back to the sign.

"It said something like "Welcome to Sanctuary, Designed by Robert, Built by Many, Made a home by Emily.""

Clint finished and looked at the General with frustration.

"Designed by Robert?" the General sneered.

"Yeah," Clint nodded. "That's what it said."

"So, you did survive, old friend," the General said to himself as he turned away from Clint.

Author's Note

Thank you for joining Emily and Marley on their journey. I hope you enjoyed their story as much as I did. If you could please review it, it would be greatly appreciated.

Are you looking for more? Please check out my other books.

Scan the QR code below for links to my social media, mailing list, and other books.

J.D. Crist

www.ingramcontent.com/pod-product-compliance
Lightning Source LLC
Chambersburg PA
CBHW011926300726
48970CB00008B/2589